a novel

by

Shawn Stewart Ruff

SugAr dAdDy

Earlier Mom announced a guest would drop by. She didn't make like it was a big surprise, but her hair was in sponge curlers and eyebrows just plucked. Us kids put our best faces on, ready as Lacey Douglas' cute sweet boys. My brothers watched the Carol Burnett Show. I could hear their easy laughter over my running bathwater. From the window just above the tub I was searching for the Big Dipper, with borrowed binoculars that had seen better days. The sky looked blacker than asphalt, the stars like scattered rock salt, and the Big Dipper just a bent barbecue fork. I bet I could more easily spot Finlater from the moon. It must be the ugliest place on earth.

I stopped searching when headlights in the parking lot caught my eye. I may not know the stars, but I do know cars. It was a fast low-rider, a fancy coupe acting like a sports car. I guessed the Thunderbird, or T-Bird, but not the new model. It was last year's, the 1968, with the cascade turn signal taillights. It was cool like Kool cigarettes. Like Smokey Robinson's "Ooo Baby Baby." The kind of car Marvin Gaye might drive.

It glided to the curb, its high beams staring at our building. It was searching for something. Or someone. What if me? But no one could ever find me, especially if they weren't from here. Our building was set on a shelf of a crabgrass hill. And Finlater had a thousand units that looked just like it.

The binoculars weren't meant for heavenly bodies. The car's interior lights showed a man I'd never seen before, a strand of gold gleaming around his neck. I watched him get out, and the headlights blink closed. He was tall. He lipped on a lit cigarette. His skin was dark and his shoes had buckles that flickered as he walked along the poorly lit sidewalk. His shirt stood out—a skintight slippery silver fabric with long sleeves. It took to moonlight like Christmas tinsel and looked brighter than the Big Dipper or any star I'd ever seen in the sky. He turned up our sidewalk, and I swear he saw me. Our eyes locked in the tug of gravity—the little body me, the big body him, in a pull like the moon toward the earth, or the earth toward the sun, or me toward fried chicken legs, my favorite thing in the world. I slumped down into bubbles, wondering about this mystery man. Was this Mom's surprise guest? What would he take from us? Some of her men took more than they gave.

The screen door yawned. A loud yelp came from downstairs. The front door banged with Mom's girlish squeals. Next I heard a man's voice shout at my brothers "Damn, Corey. Damn Dudley…" I couldn't make out what was said next. But I did hear loud feet climbing the stairs. We had only one bathroom and I was in it. I jumped up covered in bubbles, then slammed the window shut. The binoculars splashed into the bathtub just as the door pushed open. The shirt I noticed from the window was like silver fire. "Cliffy, damn." He grunted for breath. Sunglasses clamped on his head. Bourbon brown eyes fixed on me. "Shit, all y'all grown up."

He made for his zipper. I slid down into bubbles again, gripping the sides of the tub. The towel I'd put over my shoulders against the March chill now floated like a terrycloth fish.

"Stay there," he wheezed. "With any luck you inherited the good genes, and this is what you have to look forward to." He sort of laughed and coughed at the same time, breathing hard as he turned toward the toilet.

I didn't understand, but watched as his thick gold-ringed fingers unpacked his privates from tight black polyester pants. He maneuvered it until a red head came out. It looked like something Jacque Cousteau might have pulled from the deep sea. Then neon bright pee streamed out, arcing into the toilet.

"What you now, twelve?" he asked, winking at me.

"Almost fourteen," I said, watching drops fly out of the toilet like shooting stars of pee.

"Damn, I been gone that long!" he added.

He then pulled at himself, in the end squeezing until the last drops dribbled up, splattering the toilet rim. One last hard strangling shake, then he carefully repackaged it, curling it downward, cupping it like a good boy's head.

He discovered his image in the vanity mirror. He seemed pleased as he posed at different angles—smiling, unsmiling, lips puckered.

"I almost pissed my pants I had to go so bad. Just be glad I didn't have to take a shit. You wouldn't like that."

D-E-F-E-C-A-T-I-O-N spelled out in my head, and I giggled at the smelly thought. He frowned, wrinkling his upper lip.

"Bet you don't know me, do you?"

4

I shook my head no.

"Guess?"

I followed his silver shirt where it opened to chocolate muscles and the slinking gold chain. Curly, silky black hair covered his upper chest like a rug, matching that on his head and the L-shaped sideburns and goalpost mustache. His lips were purplish and like orange rind.

"Stand up."

I did.

"Don't look like you got the genes."

He shook his head, and then grabbed one of my brothers' towels, holding it open. I stepped from the tub, wondering if I should point out that the towel wasn't mine. He dried me off roughly, the terrycloth like sandpaper. Then he draped it over me and with a groan hoisted me into his arms, breathing beer smells into my face. "Give your old man some sugar," he demanded.

I was thirteen-and-a-half, five-feet-four inches tall and almost ninety-eight pounds. I couldn't remember being held like that, swept up like a little kid. His eyes marked me as his, my cheek oily where his lips kissed it.

GathEring of THe trIbeS

Sleep sometimes began with a summit. Us kids conducted business or swapped thoughts from our beds. I had the top bunk, Dudley the lower, Corey a foldaway cot. Serious issues usually meant a face to face. I would hang over the end of my bed, bat-like. Having a dad in the flesh was profound.

Corey, the youngest at eleven, was crazy-happy. His every sentence started with "Daddy said…"

"You act like you're the only kid he has," I said, ticked off. I had been spelling. I was sounding out leviathan, not for a quiz and most definitely not for another crack at the citywide spelling bee. In the final round of the last year's bee, I choked—and not on a monster of a word, but on an easy one! I had been tripped up, but still, it was a word so easy that even the neighborhood retard Mr. Denver would have gotten it right. I was done with spelling bees forever.

"Daddy's taking me to Coney Island." Corey was twisting his army men into wrestlers.

"Coney Island, Coney Island, Coney Island. Don't you ever think about anything else?" I said.

"Yeah, Disney Land."

"He ain't taking you or us nowhere," Dudley snapped. Dudley was the oldest at fifteen and was always quick with a judgment. Upside down, I could see his nose flare like a cobra neck. Out of all of us, he would remember, since he was six when our dad disappeared.

8

"What you got against him?" I asked.

"He's a jerk."

"Why you say that?"

"Mind your own beeswax 'cause curiosity killed the cat."

Dudley said kooky, cryptic things like that.

"Cliffy, he's a orphan, that's what his problem is. Who he look like?"

Corey had our dad's pretty-boy genes—the burnt sugar coloring and the flirty curly eyelashes. I looked like Mom, and Dudley like neither of them, with his big nose and freckly skin. Corey waved a five-dollar bill Dad had given him. I thought this was the real sticking point.

Corey egged on. "How much you get?"

"Chicken neck, I don't want his damn money."

"That's 'cause you ain't get none, orphan."

Dudley jabbed, "You'll see."

The fiver was to be shared. We learned that only after Corey spent it on a Hot Wheels Corvette and Reese's candy. At the time I didn't know what to think of our dad. I was lost in the arms that picked me up, the slippery lips that kissed my cheek, the itchy sideburns my own lips had touched, and Mom's chirps darting into our room like parakeets. I fell asleep hearing their feet clapping the stairs and Mom's door closing. I wondered if this was how Beaver on TV felt. Maybe we could be happy like them.

At breakfast, Mom's smile was private and shy. I'd seen that look in her eyes once before. Another man had ducked out our house early one morning. Only then her eyes had tiptoed away in embarrassment. Our one and only TV was missing, and we wondered why. This time was different, though Dad left in the middle of night.

"When's Dad taking us to Coney Island?" Corey said.

"Summer." Mom's slender lips smiled at us. The ends of her thick brown hair upturned like jays. "I didn't want to say anything about him coming in case he didn't make it."

"He's coming back?" Corey sounded alarmed.

"Yes." Mom looked at me. "Cliffy, whatcha think?" She spooned cereal into her mouth. She turned toward Dudley, as he excused himself and went to the bathroom. I could see the hickies on her neck. Her hand rearranged her hair to cover them up.

"He's nice," I said. "But what about Mr. Porter?"

Mr. Porter courted our mom. He was cheese-colored, had a dead wife, a big belly, a wreath of gray hair, and a puzzling use of "why"—"why, yes," "why, no," "why, he come..."—but he loved us kids. Made sure we were always rich in pocket money.

"Mr. Porter won't be coming around anymore."

"Why, why not?"

"Because I asked him not to. It's not appropriate now that your father's back."

C-u-c-k-h-o-l-d, I spelled to myself.

She frowned. I didn't know if I had upset her. I didn't know what she meant.

We finished breakfast and talked about our schedule. All day

Corey was "Daddy this, Daddy that," and Dudley feverish with opposite, contrary thoughts. On the bus, riding to the supermarket in Avondale, I noticed Mom dreamily staring out the window. Poor Mr. Porter never inspired such a look on her face, not even after he'd given her the rent money. The bus entered ugly south Finlater, with its trash, graffiti, and rubbed-bald yards, and we saw police cars and an ambulance with lights spinning. The bus crawled along as onlookers slowed traffic. A tribe of women in housecoats and sponge curlers and hair rags held back jumpy children, and were in turn held back by police. Then everybody froze. A sheeted body was rolled out on a stretcher. While the emergency care workers put it inside the ambulance, a police car suddenly sprang into traffic. I could see a man's dipping head in the backseat. The sponge-curler women waived accusing fingers.

"Niggers," Mom hissed.

PROS AND CONS

Three weeks, and Dad had moved in. It seemed to happen in secret and without warning. He would show up past our bedtime, so mostly we didn't see him, just the beer cans, chocolate wrappers, and weird smells left in his wake. Sometimes I would hear them moaning and grunting. Just like the cats now out in the bushes behind our building, freed at last from harsh winter.

Our biggest clue was the laundry. Bright, tight clothes regularly flapped on the clothesline, upstaging our Salvation Army shirts and pants. Mom always did wash before and after food shopping on Saturdays. She displayed his clothes like they belonged to a prince. Shirt labels were French or Italian or foreign-sounding. The materials slinky to the touch. Polyester pants flared outward in sharp creases and fabric like fancy bed sheets. The underwear was very Malibu-beach-looking, in bikini stripes, blues, reds, and yellows. By the fourth week the clothes got practical. Blue work uniforms and beside them white cotton briefs with stubborn pee and shit stains.

Still, Mom seemed to deliberately delay telling us what was obvious. Sometimes you just had to say a thing. Saturday morning, she did just that but in a roundabout way. She was filling our bowls with Sugar Snacks cereal and going over chores and the day's plans when Dudley tested her.

"I don't know which of you peed on the toilet rim, but Cliffy, you be sure to bleach it good."

It was my turn to clean. I knew whose pee it was but said

nothing.

"Where's our daddy?" Corey blurted out.

"He had a job interview at the post office," she said. "He's trying to make more money. Wish him luck."

"Okay. Good luck, Dad," Corey shouted. Sometimes he acted so retarded.

"If he gets it, he's going to stay awhile. Won't that be nice?"

"He's already been staying awhile," Dudley grumbled under his breath.

Mom heard him. Dudley chewed his lips.

"That's right, he has. I'm an adult, in case you didn't realize that. And I'm tired. It'd be nice to have things, and then I wouldn't have to work like a dog to keep it all going. Everything wouldn't be on me."

Dudley's face was a knuckle now, and Mom's voice cracked. "I need help. I can't do this by myself anymore. I just can't."

Dudley shot back, "We don't need his kind of help. What kind of daddy abandons his family and then shows up with a six-pack of Colt 45? Where he been?"

If nothing else, it confirmed Dudley knew things we other kids didn't. I guess he had a right to answers. I was also impressed that he could and did take on Mom, but I didn't like it. I wanted him to remember us all waiting an hour for the bus to carry us home from the Salvation Army clinic during a snowstorm. We were too broke to hire a cab, too beat to walk the mile or so out of Norwood to Evanston. Norwood was the white neighborhood where the Salvation Army clinic and the Klan were. Evanston, the rough black neighborhood where pity would be taken on us and a ride, plus drugs and anything else you could think of, would be offered. We were in the jam in the first place because Corey had a bad ear infection. He whimpered in a sickly way as the cold shook Mom apart and the snow blinded us. It drove at us so hard I clung to Mom to hold her together. Her eyes stared into Corey's nappy cap, the snow coating her eyelashes. Her lips looked stuck together, and it seemed like she wasn't breathing. I got really scared, I was so cold and my toes felt crushed by the numbness. Dudley spotted the #47 bus at the moment Mom seemed about to lose it, with Corey whimpering louder and louder. I was never so happy to see a bus in my life. But then, through tears I watched the bus go into a skid. Dudley and me lunged out the way, but Mom and Corey didn't move. It was like the bus headlights had pinned them to the bench. "Mom!" Dudley screamed. I could see her eyes get bigger as the bus' angled front tires slid into the curb, its huge body wobbling with all its metal blubber. But she didn't seem frightened or shaken or anything. We struggled onto the bus. The blaze of heat instantly melted the snow coating us into puddles and streams around our sneakers. Ice beads and frost and slush smeared the window. The driver fussed about the treacherous conditions, while Mom buried whimpering Corey in her damp arms, shaking and crying. I'll never forget that look on her face. I'll never forget what the driver said—"Lady, why in hell didn't you move? You almost got killed." She didn't say a word.

So I believed Mom's defense of our dad: "Your father's been in California. He was over there in Vietnam and he was drafted..."

"Mom, he left us before that, I remember. Grandpa..."

"That was a long time ago."

"We don't need him..."

"Yes, we do. Everybody deserves a second chance. Now, you hear me good, Dudley Wayne Douglas, you better not be acting ugly in front of your father. You got that?"

His jaws chomped down on bad words nobody wanted to hear.

"You boys are my men, and that's never going to change. You never have to worry about that." Her eyes gathered us up, one at a time, then all at once.

"I hope he gets the job, Mom," I said.

He did. Any doubts about his living with us were officially removed when Dad himself told us about his plans a week or so later.

We'd just come home from grocery shopping at A&P in Avondale. Mom had indulged us—from Sugar Pops and Cracker Jacks, to Snickers and chocolate chip ice cream—plus huge platters of steak and pork chops, several whole chickens and two Colt 45 six-packs, all for Dad. I guess us kids had been bribed. It worked. The one time we were too broke to afford dinner made me obsessed with food—that sorry night I was forced to chew on a freshly picked booger to calm my riled stomach. Had I not called Grandpa Pleasant, with my gut chanting in my ear, I was sure we would have died. Next day, sweet grandpa made like he just happened to come by with food and money. Mom was too embarrassed and then too relieved to question us. She swallowed her pride with a glass of Tang, courtesy of Grandpa. It was a different kind of relief with Dad, and I guess Grandpa couldn't satisfy her deeper hunger. I just wanted the bounty that came with Dad to continue. For that alone I loved him or believed I could—I never wanted to go hungry again. Still, I was surprised to see him sitting on the sofa in his exotic underwear, legs cocked open, his attention glued to a bowling tournament on the fuzzy, crackling RCA. Like he'd been there all along, a daddy centerfold in our living room, only we hadn't noticed.

"Hey Lacey," he said. To us, "How's my boys?"

"Daddy," Corey beamed and ran for a hug. "I'm glad you're back. I told everybody we got a daddy, but I wasn't sure."

"Sure am, and you got a daddy alright. I'm here to stay." He leaned toward the TV as a bowler rolled a two-pin split. "Where they get this clown from. I can bowl better than that."

A thrill went through me as I ran to the cab for more groceries. Sucking his teeth, Dudley brought the last of the bags in. One busted open as he passed the kitchen table, its contents exploding on the floor. Beer and glass shattered into a foaming piss-colored puddle. Mom ran over to Dudley and immediately managed the mess. Dudley froze. It was like he was afraid.

Our father looked up, "Shit, did they all break?"

"No," Mom said, avoiding looking at us as she swept glass

and beer into a dustpan.

"Damn, we should strain the glass out. I'll drink it."

"Oh, Cliff, I don't think so."

"You know they selling beer in cans now. Why you didn't buy that?" He stared at Dudley. "Clumsy Dudley there, bring me one and don't drop it!"

Dudley stared at Mom.

"Boy, money don't grow on trees around here."

Dudley's eyes glassed over, but he did as he was told. He didn't have to voice how pissed he was. His foul muffled words stunk the smell was so strong.

The new household was made official later that night. I was woken up by music and laughter and shouting. Us kids all seemed to rouse at the same time. Our sleepy eyes groped around for meaning, and we in order of birth and bravery headed toward the stairs, where Otis Redding and cigarette smoke and fried chicken wings smells rushed like a great wind. Corey said wow, and darted downstairs. Dudley and I cautiously crept far enough that we could see the treeline of hairdos of the churning party of 15 people or so. Big cotton candy Afros and men in Sly & the Family Stone-style cool caps, darting and jabbing hips and hands in the air. In the middle of them all, there was Dad. I saw Corey launch onto his hip, and the two cha-cha'ed their way through the crowd to the record player. Dad lifted the needle up, then talked over the suddenly peeved guests.

"Hey, everybody, here are my boys. This is Corey"—he

pointed our way—"and that's Cliffy and Dudley."

"Get out of here," one of the dudes said.

"Shit, that's what I said. They all grown up."

"Cliff, man, how many kids you got anyway?"

Dad laughed, "These all I know about. All I love. Me and Lacey's clan. My boys."

He stared our way: "Come on over here."

Dudley and me looked at each other, and then we stood up from our spot on the steps. For some reason I looked down. Dudley had a hard-on. He was the one with our father's genes, it seemed to me, as he slid his hand down to cover up.

We sidled our way through the party. Mom, in high heels and a banana-yellow miniskirt, sort of met us halfway. The music went full blast, and Dad, with Corey holding his hand, boogied our way. We all seemed to meet in the middle of the room at the same time.

Mom said, "One dance and it's back to bed."

"Lacey, let the boys have a little fun."

"That's right," Corey shouted.

"Alright, five songs."

We danced together, stepping the mashed potato, bump and hustle. And laughing—at a spinning Corey, at a big-butt lady I'd never seen before whose skirt was caught in her panties, and at the great time we were suddenly having.

When the music went off, Dad said, "Dudley, we need a DJ. Can you handle it?"

Almost against himself, Dudley grinned and rushed over to the record player.

We stayed up until the party was over. Next morning, Corey spoke for us all when he said, "See, ain't it nice having a daddy?" Not even Dudley could break the spell.

Bygones were bygones.

WOMEN IN LOVE

Us kids appearing better off set tongues wagging. Saturdays, the car swelled with groceries and family togetherness, Dad at the wheel, listing rightward in pimp style and behind sunglasses like gold plates. Mom sunken into the front bucket seat, the April wind tearing at her hair. Ford commercials didn't envision us in Thunderbirds, and neither did Dad. I guess we stunk because he loaded up on the evergreen air fresheners and we weren't allowed to move once inside the spongy upholstery. He wouldn't have let Mom drive even if she knew how. Us kids didn't complain, and neither did she. Riding a city bus was punishment enough, even in the sweet-smelling spring. Plus, all Finlater saw us speed by. A fine dad and a fine car, too.

It was mostly moms and their kids in Finlater. Dads were in short supply, and seasonal like the holidays. Having a man around carried weight and earned respect. Nice white women like Mrs. Kavanaugh congratulated Mom on Dad in wordless ways, a sponge cake or tin of cookies arriving for no good reason. Mom had joined their elite club of married women. She had never given up her married name, and I'd heard her volunteer that her husband was in Vietnam, even though the war had ended. Now she had proof the tiny sparkle on her finger wasn't for show. Mrs. Kavanaugh's dessert gesture touched Mom the most, although us kids had had better cupcakes. She lived across the front courtyard with her five pretty blond daughters. Her husband died of a stroke on the job a year ago. Mr. Kavanaugh was butterball fat and pinkish with hairs cross-stitching his ears. Finlater began as a WPA project created by President Roosevelt for poor white people, but was crumbling into a ghetto for fatherless families and alone old people. Mr. Kavanaugh was a pillar of the community, like a wise elder for a lost tribe of jilted women and their bastard children. Mom said he was just like Grandpa Pleasant—"a good, good man." The whole community mourned his passing, queued up in the rain under spindly umbrellas to pay respects at the Finlater Recreation Center.

The white lady I did chores for—who also had loaned me the lousy binoculars—wasn't impressed with our dad. Frau Zelpha Crites lived in the corner of our building, on the second floor, her bedroom touching mom's, for over twenty years. She knew the women whose husbands died in World War II or just deserted their families. She seemed to have seen everybody who came and went, as well as everybody who'd come and gone. It was her opinion that nice white families and responsible fathers fled when the "reckless" women and all their bastards started moving in. Mom couldn't stand a nosey busybody like Frau Crites, but she also felt sorry for her. She was seventy, C-O-R-P-U-L-E-N-T, with bleeding, stinky ulcers on legs that couldn't negotiate the three flights of stairs and fifty yards to transportation for food or anything. She was also a German with a thick accent, and two world wars were proof you couldn't trust those people. She was mostly alone except for my regular visits and a local charity that checked on her weekly.

"Your mom has man?" Frau Crites said, accusingly.

"He's family." I didn't want to get into it with her. I wanted the peanut butter brownies she always made for me, which she would watch me eat with watery eyes and growling stomach. And I wanted her to make Mom's birthday cake, which she said she would.

"Liebschen, don't lie. I don't like le-eng."

"I'm not lying. He's family."

"I hear zem at night. Ooo, aaah, ooooo, all night long, I hear zem."

"He's my dad."

"Dad!" She sniffed, pursing her sausage-plump lips. "He's no dad. He's a child. A man-child. You more a man than he is. He break your mother's heart. The schwartze with big pee-pees is the reason for all these black children without fathers. Look at his underwear, you'll see."

"It's wienershitzel."

"Vulgar, clever boy," she grinned, and then laughed with jiggling cheeks.

She had a point about the underwear. According to the laundry blowing on the clotheslines, nobody's dad in our part of Finlater wore such fancy drawers. The other thing she was right about was "Black women with no men" loved a fine "schwartze." They flashed for our dad, shunting their kids aside for him to see their swinging hips and titties. Mom was disgusted. She had little good to say about Finlater in general, but used to take pride in pointing out that at least there weren't Niggers in our part of the neighborhood. By 1970 all Finlater was turning black, and now two

26

courtyards away their presence was real, although mostly they still herded south of us. Mom and the other pioneer black ladies nearby couldn't stand them, with their "roaches, rats, foul country mouths, rudeness, thieving, crime, and nasty out-of-control kids busting windows and spray-painting their African-sounding names nobody could pronounce on every-damn-thing. Even if you are a Nigger you don't have to act like one"—that's how one of the ladies put it. Mom saw herself as an example. Though she had Dudley at fifteen, and had to drop out of school, she was married, always kept her kids, house, and yard clean, and spoke like a good colored woman who knew her tenses, plurals, and prepositions. And she certainly wasn't chasing after anybody else's man! Her Finlater friends thought exactly the way she did, with similar stories and skin coloring. Yet somehow Mom never seemed to notice the hunger in their eyes when Dad was around.

"Those women" weren't Mom's only problem. Grandpa and Grandma Pleasant and Mom's sisters shared Frau Crites' feelings about Dad. News of his return reached Grandpa and Grandma in Nashville. They were visiting Grandpa's cousin Remus, on his last legs from Lupus. Mom's older sister Gloria started the rumor mill turning. She provoked an argument when she heard Mom was seeing Dad again. "Lacey, why don't you marry that nice Mr. Porter; he's such a good man. Why you got to get back with that loser?" Gloria's husband was an undertaker and a family man, but an ugly buck-toothed one, and their oldest boy was on his way to Howard University, because "that's what a good man does for his kids."

All Mom could say was "He's changed. I love him. I have always loved him. He's the man for me. I can't change that, Gloria. I tried. Why can't you all just support me in this. Please. Just try."

Later, Mom sniffled and teared-up on the phone with Grandpa, no match for big P-A-T-E-R-F-A-M-I-L-I-A-S. We didn't go to their house for dinner the first Sunday they got back. Plus Mom told us not to mention Dad to Grandpa and Grandma, period. That didn't bode well for Mom, since she was, as she liked to say, a "daddy's girl."

BiRDs Of pARaDise

Us kids always pooled our money together for Mom's birthday present. Since more of our family was against Dad than for him, I figured we should get her something real special. Only we were fifteen dollars short for the 8-piece pots-and-pans set I had decided on, thanks to my no-count brothers.

"Y'all lowdown," I said. "What do we do now?"

"Ask Dad," Corey said.

"Oh hell no," Dudley said, newly soured to our dad. "I ain't sharing nothing with him."

"Sharing!" I huffed. "You put in two-dollars and fifty-cents each. You're lucky your name will be on the gift at all."

I was ready to throw a handful of pennies at them, only we had none to spare. They were playing Monopoly on Corey's bed, and so mostly talked to each other. I stewed in my top bunk, stuffing nickel, dime, and quarter wrappers, wishing we could somehow cash-in the game board money. I didn't know what to do. It was probably too late to enlist Dad anyway, since the birthday was tomorrow.

"Don't matter," Dudley shrugged.

"Huh? Don't matter if your name's on it? But it does matter if Dad gives money so we can get something nice?"

"It's the principle of the thing."

"Principle?"

"Yeah, the Nigger won't be around long enough, no how."

"He's just mad because Mom forgot his birthday," Corey

pressed his finger firmly on one of Dudley's many buttons.

"Shut up." Then, more to me than to Corey, Dudley said, "Serves her right that we only got a fifteen-dollar gift."

"She didn't forget," I said, lying. I felt bad for Mom and for Dudley that she forgot. "She had to work late."

"Yeah, right."

"And you got your cake, so what if it was on the weekend. So what."

"Chicken butt." Corey snickered.

"We have nothing to give Mom because of you two," I said. "We were each supposed to have ten bucks, remember."

"Things happen." Dudley smirked. "Pea brain, where's your ten?"

"Same place yours is."

And they both cracked up.

"It ain't fair," I went on.

"We sorry, Cliffy," Corey made like he was about to cry. "Don't be mad at us."

Corey then whispered to Dudley, making some comment that seemed to annoy him. Dudley playfully tapped Corey's head and jumped up, tipping the game board over. Corey shrieked, and Dudley gave him the finger on his way out of the room. Coast cleared, Corey rocketed from the bed and climbed the ladder into my super-hero space, poking his head just above the mattress. I thought I heard Mom shout from downstairs, but my attention was immediately grabbed by the twenty-dollar bill Corey threw on my

Batman bed sheet and the "I'm-the-man" look in his eyes.

"Where you get that?"

"From Dad. I didn't want the Rottweiler to rip it up."

"Wow. Did you tell Dad about the party?"

"Sure did, I told him the fat white German lady next door makes killer cakes."

"Did he say he'd be here for the party?"

"No, but he said he had something planned, too."

I pictured Mom and Dad dancing together, her in a big showstopping Ginger Rogers number, and him in a Fred Astaire tuxedo, with champagne waiting at their table in some fancy club downtown. My dream gift idea was a sparkly dress by a lady named Pauline Trigérè that mom and me saw featured in the newspaper. Mom savored it as the "perfect stylish dress," but it would have blown our budget for the next twenty years, even if my brothers were capable of following through with their contributions—which they weren't.

"This'll be the best birthday Mom's ever had." I gave him three dollars in rolled coins. "You're in charge of the ice cream. Get Butter Pecan. That's what Mom likes."

Just then, Mom shouted upstairs for us to go to bed before Frau Crites started banging the pipes because of the noise we were making. It's not us, I thought to myself, that makes Frau Crites mad.

Dudley came in just then. "He's here. The car just come in the parking lot."

"How you know?" said Corey. "I thought you were in their beating your meat. I heard you, Dud. Un-un-unununununnnnnnnnn."

"Funny."

They practically laughed themselves to sleep, almost the instant they quieted down, as if switched off. That was surprising because they both seemed so revved up by our dad's presence, but there they were, snoring away, in Dudley's bed. Corey still sometimes had nightmares and they would sleep together, just like in the days before he had his own cot, curled around each other like alley cats.

Next morning I told Mom I had an errand to run. I didn't say where, and she didn't ask. If she had, I would tell the truth. But she didn't because we all liked to pretend there was a real surprise to this yearly ritual. Us kids' birthdays were different. It was all on Mom to organize everything—which is partly how she forgot Dudley's 15th, and why none of us reminded her, including the miserable birthday boy himself. Moms were supposed to remember these things. That's the way things were.

I decided not to go to our usual bus stop, but to one a little out of the way, to the north of us, to avoid being seen. I went clear up toward the northern edge of Finlater, where we knew no one— and where, beyond the Finlater Recreation Center, another neighborhood began. I could see the bus coming, and I ran to reach the stop in time. I grinned at the driver as I plopped in the fifteen-cent fare, as if to say, Yes, I ride the bus alone all the time. I eyed the aisle and the back of the bus. It was empty now, but would soon fill with Finlater folks, mostly with whites at first, but by the time we reached the end of Finlater, it would be weighed down with young, loud, cursing black folks. Mom always insisted on the front seats, after years of Jim Crow laws that denied black folks such prime locations. Civilized people sat in front, and bad people in the back, she told us. If the front seats were all taken, she'd do a quick survey. If it was a rout back there, we'd stand in front, unless she was pretty worn-out or weighted down with stuff—and even then she rode in total disgust, her hand over her mouth as if she were about to throw up.

I sat upfront with the old ladies, ignoring the sneers and snickers of the kids boarding. This was my first trip downtown without a grownup or my brothers, and nothing was going to take away my excitement. Even south Finlater looked beautiful to me now. Avondale and Clifton might have been world-class cities, the way my heart beat.

Once downtown, I raced to Shillitoe's, and pushed through those giant revolving doors into heaven. Housewares was in the basement, I knew, but that wasn't my first stop. Now that there was the possibility Dad was taking Mom out, I couldn't get the Pauline Trigérè dress out of mind. With luck maybe I'd find a nice manager who would say, You can take that 150-dollar dress for 32 bucks just because you're such a nice kid to want Pauline Trigérè for your mom's birthday.

I found the floor where thousands of ladies clothes were. I always loved Shillitoe's and watching Mom try on dresses, even as my brothers flipped out. Mom stopped trying on clothes after Corey and Dudley somehow managed to knock an entire carousel over.

One flight up, a world of evening gowns and fancy la-di-da stuff. Mom never went further than four, so I did now, just to see. There, I pawed every glittery, sparkly, furry thing I saw. I pulled a couple size fours from the rack and ran my fingers over fabric just to touch it, and then sniffed the smell of rich newness. White ladies stared at me, and I smiled like I belonged here.

"May I help you?" A tall, suited man was suddenly standing behind me. His eyes seemed closed, and set in wrinkles like quotation marks.

"Hi sir, I'm looking for a dress for my mom's birthday. It was in the paper two weeks ago. It's by Miss Pauline Triger-ee."

"That's Tree-zsher." His boomerang eyebrows lifted, the robin's-egg blue eyes opened fully, shifted to their corners. He smiled a little, with movie-star teeth. "That's designer sportswear."

"Where's that?"

"Over there," he said, pointing a crooked finger decked out in sparkly stones like something Liberace might wear.

He leaned down to me. "Listen darling, you're an adorable little Negro—I can see that (he winked)—and I know you ain't here to steal, but I don't think you belong here, or in designer sportswear for that matter. All these old bitches are complaining. Now go on down to the Missy Floor where it's okay for you people to shop. Ask for Barbara, she'll help. Have a nice day."

"But I…"

"Now run along."

I did—pissed off and scared of what I didn't know, and feeling better the instant I was away from him. My love of Shillitoe's suddenly faded. I went to Housewares with my lower lip trembling. Yesterday I had called to ask them to hold one 8-piece cookware advertised special, and they said yes, but nobody had done it and they were now sold out. The manager—a shiny old lady with a white mustache—said, "Hon, the best I can do is give you one of these cast-iron sets. It's got fifteen pieces."

"I only have thirty-two dollars."

"You got a good deal, then. It's $25.99."

She had a stock person roll out a 15-piece cast iron cooking set.

"Wow," I said, staring at the soup pot and pancake griddle. Better than any old Pauline Tree-chair-ee dress. I gave mister-movie-star-teeth the invisible finger.

It wasn't until I rolled the shopping cart to the exit that I realized I had a big problem. It wasn't just that the box was wider than my arms were long. Its weight was 35 pounds, or so the box said. I struggled wrestling it out of the cart. I didn't make it to the end of the block before dropping it, with such a racket people stared. The bus stop was two blocks away. How was I going to get there? I looked around for help. There was an alley that cut through the block, and I could see the backdoor to Newbury's, our favorite five-and-dime for hamburgers and milkshakes after our good behavior while Mom shopped. I teetered and strained with my heavy box, and wasn't far into the trash-filled shortcut when I heard footsteps. I didn't see the stringy-haired muggers until I was grabbed from behind, the box snatched from me, and a fist hit me in the stomach. Both were white—that much I could tell from my fetal position as I moaned on the ground, where I was thrown after one of them went through my pockets. I helplessly watched them get away with Mom's birthday present.

No bus fare, and no way home, and no way to call Mom to tell her what happened. I didn't know what else to do but go back to the Shillitoe's and beg for another gift.

I was about to do just that when I heard: "Young man, young man, u-whooooo!"

It was mister-movie-star teeth.

"I'm sorry for what happened earlier," he said.

I shivered. I hardly heard him, I was so in shock and in pain.

"These old biddies never change." He smiled. "Hey, what's wrong? Are you alright?"

"No," I blubbered. "I got jumped. They took my mom's birthday present and my money, too."

"Poor dear little boy. It's just terrible downtown. Where's your mom now?"

"I came by myself to get the birthday present."

"How brave. Why, I'm scared to death just walking to the parking lot! Are you hurt?"

"I'm okay, sir."

He petted my head. "And so deliciously… Why, if you were only a little older…"

He reached into his pocket. "Here's some bus fare." He handed me a dollar. Then, looking at a little shopping bag he was carrying, he said, "Your mom got a man?"

"Yeah," I said.

"Then she'll love this."

He handed me the bag.

"I was just meeting a girlfriend for lunch to give it to her, but I can get another one. You take it—consider it a gift from Shillitoe's. You come down here again, you let me know how she likes it. Now run along before something else happens to you."

"Thank you, sir."

And I thanked the God in Heaven—because that's what we do when good things happen. I was so relieved my stomach stopped hurting. On the bus, I peeked into the bag and saw what looked like lace, feathers, and silk. Whatever it was, I didn't dare pull it out in front of everyone. And this much I knew—the thing was either going to get me punished or kissed, never mind anything else I had done today. Once off the bus, I ran home, almost desperate to see the creature in the bag.

A pre-screening wasn't to be. The party was underway, just waiting for me to show up.

"There you are, where have you been?" Mom beamed.

"I…"

"Your father has to work early today. Corey went and got the cake—that was awfully nice of Mrs. Crites."

"Cliffy, my boy, we were just about to start without you." Dad poured champagne into Mom's glass. There was a big bouquet of flowers on the table—roses with baby's breath. The cake Frau Crites baked was there too, with candles burning, spreading a scent of warm vanilla sugar.

"Here's some Coke for you boys," Dad said, pouring out glasses. "Let's sing for your mom."

We all sang, our voices cracking, off pitch, Corey howling the words "…and many more."

Mom glowed. She kissed Dad and all us kids.

Dad handed her a little box, adding "They're real this time."

"Oh, Clifford," she cooed, after discovering sparkly earrings. She threw her arms around him. To us she explained that he gave her fake diamonds for her fifteenth birthday.

"And I couldn't even afford that," he laughed. "But I sure did love your mom even if it did break the bank."

Thinking of her as Dudley's age suddenly made me see her and Dad differently. They had been kids, just like us. I'd seen a bunch of pictures of Mom at all ages, but it was still hard to picture her wetting the bed, flying on a swing, busting whitehead pimples. Mom, as if reading my mind, said, "We were in the ninth grade. Your daddy was the first man I ever loved."

"Who the second?" Corey said.

"There's no second." Her eyes sparkled even more than the diamond earrings, and I believed her. "He's the first and the last."

"Your mama was the prettiest girl at school," Dad said. "She's the prettiest girl still, especially round here, that's for damn sure."

"And the winner is, Miss Finlater 1970 goes to Lacey Douglas," Corey said.

"Oh, Corey," Mom blushed.

"What you boys get your mom?" Dad said.

"I… um…" I handed Mom the bag.

She teased the thing out, eyes widening in a visible blush. It was a hoe-nightie, its feathers fluttering in the air, the black see-through top dangling leopard printed panties. "My goodness. Cliffy, what in the world…"

Corey and Dudley clapped hands over their mouths. I swallowed Coke, choked on the bubbles. I would just keep my saga to myself, I decided right then and there on the spot.

"Ooo baby baby," Dad said, handing Mom the cake knife. "We'll make good use of this. Cliffy, you done good. I think I'll get your advice on lady gifts from now on."

DADDY ENVY

I kept my dad a secret awhile. Kids without dads are desperate and jealous. Those with dads can be uppity and sharp. My best friend Delrico was the first person I told. My admission to Frau Crites didn't count since she figured it out.

I told Delrico only because he saw my dad leaving our place, and I had to say something. I felt sorry for Delrico. His family was from New York, but his dad was murdered by Cleveland police and his mom was a Puerto Rican doing time for robbery. Delrico had accidentally killed his baby sister. The story his brother Santiago told us was, Delrico was four years old when he fed his sister cereal with pretty blue Drano sprinkles, while their mother was out partying. Santiago had gone to the store for sugar, and later found his siblings sprawled on the floor, Delrico bent over the dead baby as blue bubbles gathered around her mouth. Now the brothers lived in Finlater with their daddy's mother, Miss Tussy, who made Delrico carry a wallet-size picture of his poisoned sister, shot daddy, and jailbird mom, so he wouldn't forget. It was such a heavy burden his pants always sagged.

"Must be nice having a daddy," he said.

"It's alright. He watches TV all the time and makes out like us kids are waiters in a restaurant. Get this, get that."

"You mind?"

Did I? "Guess not. He got grazed by a bullet in Vietnam, and that scared the bejesus out of him."

"He ain't mean though?"

"Nope. I don't know. He's kinda funny. But he drinks a lot of beer and… I don't know, seem like he could be mean."

"I don't remember my dad none, but my mom, she was real mean. Whupped us all the time."

"He's mostly nice, I think. He and my mom were junior-high school sweethearts."

"Wow."

Neither of us had sweethearts, and we were in junior-high, so it seemed pretty deep, to me at least. I wonder if I would have a sweetheart. A love like Mom's for Dad. She would have to have really long hair. I liked hair.

"We'll be getting our own house."

"You moving?"

"Probably."

"I hope you don't move far away."

"Me, too."

It seemed too sophisticated to talk about my dad's bikini underwear, since Delrico's was always dingy and torn up, from what I could see from Miss Tussy's clothesline, so we talked about the Thunderbird instead. Delrico thought the 1963 model was better looking. I agreed. That was the extent of our conversation about Dad.

Delrico wasn't my real best friend anymore. Not that he ever was. I just didn't have a friend I liked more before the new school year started. School sorted us by grade and by brains, and I was ahead of all my Finlater friends. Delrico was thirteen, too, but was held back a year and so was in the sixth grade. He wasn't a quick learner, even with his Coke-bottle-thick eyeglasses, a werewolf hairline, and pointy ears, yet he was a saxophone whiz, able to listen to radio tunes and then play them back on that instrument. School bored him though, and he had failed fourth grade. Maybe it was just hard to get excited about anything once you committed murder, accident or not. I always thought he looked less like a killer and more like a communist, even though I didn't know one to compare him to. Delrico just seemed like a communist—quiet, a little scary, beady-eyed, the dust-colored hair, and tiny teeth. Anybody who could kill and not remember it, or who pretended not to remember, must not be very smart, and could be a communist, I figured. I felt sorry for him.

Noah Baumgarten was my real best friend, although I didn't tell him about my dad, either. Noah lived in Elmwood, where our school was. It was a three mile walk from Finlater, and the houses there were the color of Easter eggs—lemon yellow, canary blue, and light green or just plain white. Our new house had to be near him, so we could be together all the time. Next year Noah was going to attend a school for super smart kids. And so was I.

Noah and I met in algebra the first day of the new school year. I had been called into the school administrator's office just before lunch. Over the weekend, someone had tagged in silver spray paint the school entrance with PLANET OF THE APES, which prompted NIGGERS BELONG IN ZOOS in black, which earned a blood-red YOUR MAMA. My first thought was I was in trouble, only I hadn't done anything wrong. Then I thought something bad had happened to Mom again. Last year she had had to be rushed to the hospital for an emergency appendectomy—which at first excited me because I liked science and medicine words, the real test of a good speller. The school summoned us kids and kept us there in the principal's office until Grandpa arrived, but by then I was freaked out that Mom was really sick and might die.

Principal Schor was a short, hairy, wiry man with eyebrows that bushed over the rim of his eyeglasses. He had little to say and always seemed rushed and lost in his thoughts. Sometimes he'd nod and wave while passing through the playground or down the halls. This was his second year at Elmwood, and school had changed. Within three weeks of his arrival, me and three other black kids were pulled out of the "zoo"—the classes for us black kids—and put into regular ones, and we all did well. And I did the best of all.

Turned out this new summons had a special purpose. His eyebrows wriggled like caterpillars as he congratulated me on my "outstanding performance" on the scholastic achievement test last year. I would be promoted over a grade—"I expect you to do well," he said. There was an "or else." If I didn't catch on by the end of that October, I'd be put back to seventh grade. To put the fear of God in me he said, "I thought for sure you were going to win the spelling bee last year. Of course it wasn't a trick word, it was a question of pronunciation. But still… You should have known."

Just like that, my excitement turned into a lump of protest in my throat. It really was unfair.

I was escorted to Mrs. Sovitsky's algebra class. I was depressed, sweating and burning when she said, "Class, this is Clifford Douglas." I half expected her to add, "…the spelling bee flop from last year."

I was placed in the only available seat, belonging to someone out with bad poison ivy. The seat was beside Noah and temporarily broke up her alphabetical grid. Mrs. Sovitsky pointed out that Noah and I were wearing the same button-down striped shirt.

"Maybe you're long lost twins, separated at birth," she joked, and even I laughed at the idea. Noah grinned a smile of braces, and after class said, "Hey, cool shirt. Bet you got it at my dad's store."

"Bet not." Unless his dad owned the Salvation Army. We pushed our way outside class into the main hall.

"It's Ben's, right?"

"I don't know," I said. I wasn't going to admit where it came from.

"Let me see the label." His long creamy fingers reached for my neck, and I couldn't stop the giggles. "Sears!" he shouted. He made like he was puking, then stuck out his tongue. The braces made his teeth looked wrapped in tin foil, and his red lips dry and chafed with pain. His green-bean-colored eyes had sleep crust in their corners, as if he'd run from bed straight to school without washing. Thick, heavy, wavy bangs hung down his forehead. He flung his head to the side like he was having seizures. The hair whipped upward, then collapsed around his head again in a shaggy heap.

I offered that "My mom knows all about Ben's though."

"Everybody knows about Ben's. My dad's store's the best men's store in downtown Cincinnati, in business since 1906. I bet your dad knows."

"I bet he does, too."

My dad hadn't showed up yet, but I never really wanted a dad as much as I did right then, just to say that mine knew Ben's store. Like Mom, I didn't divorce Dad from my story and told everyone he was in the military. Everyone except Noah. I let him believe that my dad was working out West, doing something in Arizona, working on a secret project that would save the world. In history class we talked about Los Alamos, and we all knew big nuclear bombs that saved the Allied Forces from the Axis Powers were created there.

"Wow," Noah said.

"What's your dad's name?"

"Clifford Romel Douglas."

"You named after him?

"That's right."

"I'm a junior, too. Noah Ben Baumgarten."

"We're twins in that way, too."

"I'm gonna tell my dad about Clifford Romel Douglas and if your mom wants to buy a present for your dad, I'm sure he'll give her a discount on the finest men's clothing in town. My dad marched on Washington in 1963 for civil rights for black people. My dad says Jewish and black people have a history of oppression together."

"I didn't know that." Which was true, although it seemed to me that I never heard the word "Jewish" until now. Maybe they were another kind of Nigger, only they didn't look like it. How many kinds of Nigger are there, I wondered?

"We're soul brothers."

"Cool."

"Maybe your dad'll have some neat souvenirs, some plutonium or kryptonite…"

"Yeah, maybe. It's top secret so…"

"You into the Jackson Five?"

"Yeah, and I like the Beatles, too."

"Cool, soul brother. From now on you're SB."

I laughed, it sounded so weird. He held out his hand for a ritual handshake he seemed to expect me to know, and then threw his arm around my shoulder.

After school I introduced him to Delrico and my brothers. But the gang wasn't as excited about Noah as I was. It was an Elmwood bias, an us-against-them way of thinking, and just plain old jealousy. Delrico sucked his tiny teeth: "What that white sheet boy hanging out with you for?" "Blacks and Jews have shared oppression," I said. Dudley's hackles went straight up—"Elmwood boys get their asses kicked in Finlater." Plus, Dudley didn't take my skipping a grade too well. He was barely surviving eighth grade, if his fall report card was to judge. C's and D's to my A's. Noah followed us to the park untouched that day, but the next day words flew.

"Honkie, we don't like you hanging around us."

"What I do to you?" Noah said.

"It ain't what you did to me, it's what we gonna do to you. Play with fire, you get burnt."

"Where's the fire?" Noah said, picking up on my zany brother's nonsense.

"We don't want you hanging with us. Get lost."

"I'm not hanging with you, I'm with Cliffy."

I jumped between them, telling Noah to go home. Noah shouted butt hole and ran off.

"That's my friend."

"That's a white boy."

I hated Dudley the sphincter even more for that. I wouldn't say that Noah was my best friend to spite them all. But I definitely was that much more determined to be best friends. It was just like Mom saying to her sister "Can't you all just to support me in this," except Aunt Gloria wasn't a nutjob like my brothers or a murderer like Delrico.

I guess I was really my mom's son.

WET BEHIND THE EARS

Dad had been around a month by April Fools. Us soul brothers were on the same afternoon class track and were between playing pranks—"Ugh, there's bird shit in your hair" and stuff like that. We even talked about taking a boat down the Amazon. But after school, Noah suddenly seemed mad. I had to get home, and with my brothers, or else.

"SB, nothing personal, but this friendship sucks. I mean, I wish you could come to my house after school so I could show you some of the stuff my dad got in Brazil and Africa, but you're like on curfew all the time and your brothers are psycho. Why do you have to rush home?"

"My mom's just scared something'll happen to us. Finlater's rough, and Elmwood's white."

"Shoot, I wish I was black, or you were white, then we wouldn't have this problem."

"You don't want to be black."

"Why?"

"You'd really be a Nigger then."

"Yeah, well…"

"It'd be fun to be white, though. I'd get to live in a big house with a color TV in my own room. I'd get straight hair and blue eyes or booger-colored eyes like yours and my dad and mom would say smart things all day drinking martinis and eating hors d'oeuvres—H-O-R-S-D'-O-E-U-V…

"Shit, you spell better than white people and everybody… I

saw you win our school bee last year."

"You did."

"Yep. It was cool."

My stomach suddenly burned—it seemed anything to do with bees made me sick. I waited for him to bring up my citywide bee meltdown, but he didn't—maybe he didn't know—so I changed the subject.

"You been on an airplane?"

"Of course…"

"Yes, see, that's what I mean… black people can't do nothing."

"You can't fly?"

"No," I shrilled. Being broke was the same thing as race discrimination to me, definitely.

"SB, I hate white people too…"

"But you white."

"No, I ain't. I just look it. I'm a Jew, I told you. Jews ain't white."

I was confused. But maybe not. There were white people in Finlater, but they weren't real white people. They were a lesser form, white trash, because they were poor as dirt. Likewise, well-off black people were still Niggers, only grand—and I never heard of any of them that had been on planes, except for Army and Navy men being flown into war, which wasn't like going to Acapulco. So Jews could somehow be like black people, only they looked like white people, yet weren't white though they could do white things, like flying in airplanes.

"And I don't know what you're doing calling yourself black. Shoot, you ain't much darker than me. Do I call myself black because my hair is black?"

"That's true, but..."

"And you don't want to be a Jew."

"Why not? To me it looks like you got it made. A Nigger with white prerogatives."

"Prerogatives? You heard of the Holocaust?"

"Yeah."

"See, you don't wanna be a Jew. Too much work—there's a lot of holidays but it's even more work. It's sanctioned oppression, it's God's tyranny."

"Wow."

"That's my dad talking now."

Whatever it meant, it couldn't be worse than our lot. "I wouldn't mind being a Jew," I added.

"Trust me. It's no fun. But I think maybe I'd like being black. I could dance and jive-talk and fuck all day in the ghetto..."

"Can Jews say 'jeepers' and 'holy-moly' and 'gee wiz' and not get beat up? 'Cuz, if you can, then it seems like you more white than black. You get beat up for saying things like that in Finlater."

"Really? Wow." Noah bubbled. "If I were a Nigger, I could rhyme and dress like a pimp. I'd have a real big cock..."

He must have seen the shock on my face, and we laughed until we were falling over each other.

"Shoot, I just thought of something. There's a house a block away from me that your mom could get. Your mom doesn't need your dad to get a house. And hey, once your mom's in the neighborhood—it can't be worse than Finlater—we can hang out all the time."

"Wow," I said. "That's great."

"Yeah, my dad can even help."

"I'll tell my mom."

"Tell your mom to go down to my father's store and buy your dad something for Father's Day or his birthday or anything."

"She can do that."

My dilemma didn't register until much later. I could only picture Mom's excitement over the house. We could move in immediately, and become the first, and probably the only, blacks in Elmwood. Mom was proud of her pioneering days in Finlater, so she would be pleased about that. Plus, Noah's parents would love us. Noah's mom and mine would do Saturday grocery shopping together and swap recipes. Us kids could play together. Our dads... holy-moly, shit! There was the problem, the big rub. Just then, with perfect timing, Bikini Dad, with a Schlitz in hand, passed through the living room, on his way from the kitchen. The air in my hopes drained out. What if Noah had already told his dad about my superhero dad? How was I going to introduce Bikini Dad? It was just too bad I couldn't say April Fools to get off the hook.

Over dinner that night, I said nothing about the house, except to ask Mom if she was looking. Dudley ate a knuckle sandwich on the Finlater basketball court earlier, and Corey was acting ugly. Mom was in a bad mood. She said, "Cliffy, you don't just look at a house. You gotta have money. And money is what we don't have right now."

In bed, I couldn't stay asleep, my imagination building houses and a future of fun with Noah. It must have been after midnight that I heard the TV going. That was a sure sign Dad was back home. Mom made him watch TV in the living room when she had to work in the morning. I decided I was thirsty and made my way downstairs.

"Boy, what you doing thirsty at this hour?"

"Just am."

"Come here."

I did. Stopping right in front of him, close enough that I could smell Schlitz and cigarettes on his breath.

"You a pretty boy, just like your mom. That's who you take after."

"Corey takes after you."

"Lucky him," Dad winked.

They were the pretty boys. Maybe Dad meant a different pretty. I smiled, and he pulled me by the arms and squeezed me between his legs. I squirmed, it tickled, and he spun me around, pressing me against him.

"You just like her."

He kissed me on the neck, his smoky breath and mustache tickling my ears, and then pressed me against that yucky underwear. I pulled myself away, giggling. Maybe Noah's dad would like him.

He pulled me against him again, this time scissoring me between his legs, tight.

"You like having your old man around?"

"I do, Dad," I said. He scooted me onto his knee. "My friend at school, his dad owns Ben's store downtown."

"Ben's on Race street?"

"Yeah, that's the store. The best men's clothing in town, since 1906."

"My black ass! That old Jew store been ripping Niggers off since I was a boy."

"Huh?" I was shocked. "He's not ripping us off. My friend's dad marched on Washington with Martin Luther King, Jr. He's a… he's a Nigger lover. Jews are just like black people."

"A Nigger lover, huh? Just like black people, huh?" Dad laughed. "Boy, Jews own everything but a Nigger's soul, and that's only because slavery's illegal. You got a lot to learn."

"You're wrong," I nearly shouted. "Mr. Baumgarten's gonna give you money off."

"It ain't a discount if it's overpriced to begin with." He pushed me off his knee and slapped me gently on the butt. His hand grabbed at his privates.

"Don't stay wet behind the ears too long. The sooner you realize that white—and that's anybody who ain't black—mean you no good, the better off you'll be. Now, go to bed so you don't fall asleep in school tomorrow."

I could hardly sleep for the slur against Noah—my twin, my pale-faced soul brother. I realized I didn't know what a Jew was, and should probably find out, since I was now determined to become one in the face of this great opposition. But what I did know for sure was that Dad could be unpredictable and mean.

Next day, Noah busted with curiosity.

"Hey, was your mom excited about the house?"

"Yeah."

"Is she coming down to meet my dad and buy something?"

"Well, she's working really hard and trying to save every penny for the house."

He shook his head.

"But I'm sure she will."

"Yeah, I hope so. Let's go see the house right after school. You can meet my mom and we can listen to Jimi Hendrix. You like Hendrix?"

I said yes. I didn't, but knew I would if Noah did. Why, I'd even eat peas without gagging, I felt certain.

"You know I gotta go home after school."

"I know, but it's Friday, daggonnit. Maybe you could just take my bike home."

I didn't say anything.

"I got a better idea, soul brother. You can ride your bike over tomorrow. You got one?"

"Sure."

"Get it and meet me here at high noon. You can meet my dad, and we'll go look at the house. That way you know what you're talking about when you tell your mom how nice it is."

"High noon?" I said, with a John Wayne twang.

"High noon."

DIRTY RAT BASTARD

I needed to borrow Delrico's bike. Mom took her time leaving
for grocery shopping. I couldn't figure out what in the sam-hell (as
Grandpa would say) she was waiting for, and couldn't leave until
she did. She flitted about the kitchen, tending wash and frying
sausage at the same time, her hair escaping bobby pins and
flopping in her face. Corey was telling her about school open
house, and Dudley looking like a juvenile defender. Mom wasn't
paying attention to either of them, and I knew something was
wrong.

I figured Dad would give Mom cab money to the grocery
store and back, just like he had done these last few weeks. Us kids
didn't mind since it meant we were entrusted to his care. In the
beginning he tried to engage us, even once going so far as to play
football-toss with us on the front courtyard—it ended officially in a
dirt slide and a cloud of curses when he tripped in his platform
shoes while running for a pass. After that, he communicated with
the TV more than he did us, more likely to ask for a beer than
question our whereabouts. Mostly he just sprawled across the couch
or perched in his favorite chair, in his bikini underwear, feet
propped on the coffee table, ashy toes trilling and cracking.
Sometimes he just stayed upstairs. We'd then see him long enough
to deliver beer, pretzels, Fritos, or chips. Sometimes there'd be a
book curled in his lap, so totally entertaining him he wouldn't see
us kids slip by. Usually they were written by somebody named
Dashiell Hammet, with a white lady on the cover. Used to be that

you could get lynched for looking at a white lady, Grandpa and history books warned us, but what would happen if she were on a book cover?

I soon realized the problem. Dad just strolled in from a night of hanging out, judging from his tight clothes, smell of smoke and booze.

"Just in time," he burped, his eyes were webbed with bloodshot. "I'm hungry as hell. You wouldn't believe what happened to me last night."

"What happened, Daddy?" Corey shouted.

Mom didn't look too happy just then. Dad went on about a tire going flat when he was over at Fleet's Place, in Silverton.

Us kids swallowed our food and left the table.

Upstairs, Dudley said, "I don't like that drunk Nigger."

Corey said, "That's because you don't like nobody and you're a mean chicken butt orphan."

"Shut up."

"You shut up."

"Mom said we're going to get a house," Corey tossed in.

"A horror house," Dudley snapped back.

"Chicken butt, chicken butt."

"Horror house, horror house."

"I'm gonna give you another knuckle sandwich," Corey shouted, pouncing on Dudley. The two turned and tumbled and screeched and laughed. Dudley was capable of snapping boney Corey in two, and sometimes seemed as if he would. How long before the blood flowed?

I wasn't about to get stuck minding Corey, so I slipped out of the house without a word. I heard Dad say, "Come on, Lacey, baby. I even asked you to come with me last night—these kids is old enough to take care of themselves. They don't need you when they sleeping!"

Well, I for one didn't have nightmares anymore—and then mostly about being chased by big hairy, snarling dogs, and dogs weren't allowed in Finlater. And with Dad here, I never slept in Mom's bed anymore, so I guess he was right. But still, the thought of Mom not being here in the night would give me nightmares, I figured. I guess if I didn't know she wasn't here...

I could see Noah hopping mad because I was late. I partly lied to him about having a bike. I had a bike once, only it got stolen. I left it unlocked on our front stoop, and it was ripped off some time in the night. We all concluded it was the new Niggers. Now I shared Delrico's bike, available to me anytime he wasn't using it, which meant it was always available since his vision was so poor. He lived on the western end of Finlater, a short trip from our place through several courtyards. Delrico's block seemed to have the most old white ladies—always frowning from behind parted lace curtains—but their little corner of Finlater was well scrubbed and had the brightness of fresh laundry. Beyond their block was a wooded area that hid mountains of sand belonging to a cement company further west. On windy days everything was covered in dust. Delrico would wheeze and cough, and the old ladies would

64

come out with their brooms and dustpans and Windex, hankies tied over their mouths like bandits.

His grandmother answered the door. Miss Tussy's eyes were distant planets behind thick-lensed cat glasses—clearly the source of bad vision in the Washington family. Day or night she was in a housecoat, smelling like a dairy, ready for bed. She asked after my "people" and sent me to "Delly."

Their place was a two-storey like ours. Delrico's brother Santiago whizzed by me on the stairs and said "the killer's up there."

Said killer was in his room playing with his electric football set. "Hey Delly."

He sucked his teeth. "If you wanna borrow my bike, I think you shouldn't mess with me."

"What's eating you?" Delrico was a kid of moods. I didn't say where I was going on his bike, but he knew.

"Nothing's eating me."

"Come on, Del. What I do?"

"You got your secrets, I got mine."

"Okay, you loaning me the bike or not?"

"Naw."

"Then what you say I could have it for?"

"Beats me."

"Forget you then."

"Forget you back."

I gave him the finger. He gave me the finger. We had

capped each other with insults before, putting each other down for the fun of it. But this was serious and warranted cursing.

"You dried-booger, snot-nosed dirty rat bastard," I shouted and took off down the steps.

"Your daddy."

"Felon!"

"Your mama."

I hated him. If Noah left without me, I'd slash Delrico's bike tires. It was fifty minutes to Elmwood if I walked. Thirty-five if I ran. Luckily track was my sport. I was a blue ribbon winner at the 50-yard dash. Four victories so far, and one third-place in the 100, and that was because my sneaker laces tripped me up. My knee and elbow skin and blood marked the crash spot on the homestretch.

I shot straight across Finlater from Delrico's place. I ran along the backyard walks that cut between buildings and parking lots to the main roads tying the projects together. At the eastern edge of Finlater, I stood on top a small hill, a short distance from the only traffic light. It seemed like I was at a fork in the road of life. Even though I was becoming a good liar, I'd never disobeyed Mom's rules like this before.

Estee Avenue was dangerous. Traffic leaving Finlater zipped toward College Hill and western Cincinnati. Or raced toward jobs at the plumbing and electrical parts factories in the eastern part of town. Most of the rush was going to the big cement company. I knew they were thinking, "What kind of mother leaves her child to run wild in the streets?" A Finlater one. If Mom had ridden by just

then, she'd have shaken her head in disgust. I ignored all the stares
and bolted across at the first chance.

On the other side of Estee were the baseball fields I passed
on the way to school. A game was in progress. Finlater people were
not among the players. These players were citywide, their team
shirts naming the part of the city they were from—Greenhills, Blue
Ash, Wyoming, Lockland. And they were big guys with padded
thighs in tight pants, and Popeye arms. Mostly white, but black too.
I navigated around the outfield, as a fly ball hurtled my way. A
red-faced leftfielder charged toward me, shouting "Hey kid, scram."
I ran as fast as I could, turning into the woods at the first available
trail. The trail cut through teethy thickets that chewed my arms
and pant legs, and came out on the long winding path to Elmwood.

Sunlight sparkled over the treetops like stars in the sky. I
kept up my speed so white kids grass-sledding on the hillside in the
distance wouldn't see me. Elmwood had no gangs that I knew of,
but I wasn't taking any chances. I should have been tired, but I ran
faster, trying to become a blur. A magical animal with speeds
faster than the human eye could detect. On the street that led to
our school I ran so fast my legs seemed like they were growing in
my pants. I slowed down only when I was in front of our familiar
playground, all ready to speed again, to go back home if necessary.

There was no need. Noah was popping wheelies on the
school playground, on a sparkly green bike with a yellow banana
seat. The front tire turned in the air as the bike bucked, the
streamers on the handlebars swinging like ponytails.

"Ah darnit, Cliffy, where's your bike?" he shouted. His sweaty face as bright as milk, stalks of black hair pasted to his face.

"Naw, four-eyes Del changed his mind."

"Liar. I thought you said you had one."

"I did, but it got stolen because of Delrico, so now we share his bike. So it wasn't a prevarication."

"A what?"

"Pre-var-i-cay-shun."

"What the fuck is that?"

"A lie. P-R-E-V-A-R-"

"Okay, smartypants. I guess you can locomote my brother's bike. Only we have to sneak it out. Climb on."

I did. We wobbled out of the playground but got surer on Elm, turning down Oak. We went deeper into Elmwood than I'd ever gone before in my three years at the school, past houses like the ones near school, only bigger. Some were twice as tall as Finlater buildings, and as wide as three of our units. Mangy grass, bicycles, basketball hoops over garages and station wagons meant children at home.

At the corner of Oak and Fern streets I saw the biggest house I'd ever seen. As big as our whole building and five stories tall. Gleaming white, it was set back farther than the other Elmwood houses. Five lawn sprinklers tossed jets of water across the lawn, like a synchronized pissing contest in slow motion. Forty or fifty people must live there, it seemed to me. Must be grand to grow up in a place like that.

"No way, that's not the house for you."

"I didn't think you'd show me a mansion."

"A big ugly house is what it is."

"Why you say that?"

"Snooty, stuck up people. They own a brewery and my dad says they're against unions."

"Oh," I said.

A red 1966 Buick Special pulled up suddenly like it was about to run us down. But it glided to the curb instead, just as we swerved to the opposite side of the street. Three girls sprang out, in blue jean skirts and halter-tops, their skin like white clay. "Oh, cunts," Noah hissed. He slowed down and circled back, in time to see them leave the car doors open and run wild. They were all giggles and screams of delight, their shiny hair waving in the air like blond silk pennants. They ran into the lawn and danced through the sprinklers, their titties bouncing up and down as the water tickled them into laugher, their wet skin lit up like slicks of ice. At one point the three held hands and danced a circle around one of the sprinklers, while chanting song lyrics we couldn't make out, like they were doing a rain dance or something. It wasn't like the bus stop or hustle dance us blacks did, and the folks I knew in Finlater would have busted stitches laughing. But to me they were like beautiful fairies coming out of the darkness and winter cold to dance in the sunshine and greening and flowering of our little world. I had never had a Saturday like this.

"The girl with the jugs is Muriel," Noah said. "She's a

cheerleader at Xavier High. Know what a nymphomaniac is?"

"Muriel," I repeated, already drunk on her name, watching her bare pink feet and white pencil-thin legs bend and stretch in pretty skipping.

"SB, you know what a nymphomaniac is?"

I said nothing. I could spell it, but I forgot its meaning.

"That's a girl with a real hot pussy. She does guys all the time."

"Oh."

I barely heard him, and I didn't care. To live in such a house forever, or even for just this one day, would be heaven.

Noah snarled, "Girls are so stupid." He pedaled us away. I turned to watch ours jump into the car. Their car lunged into the street like a big animal. Maybe they had another date on another lawn in another part of Elmwood.

"You know what a union is?"

Turning back toward Noah, I said I didn't.

He shook the back of his head at me in disgust. "A union is an organization that protects workers' rights. SB, I think we studied unions in the seventh grade. Maybe you really should be put back a grade."

"Right, I'll go ask Mrs. Sovitsky to turn me in."

"Back with the retards."

They were not retards, just black, but I didn't correct him. I instead said, "My mom belongs to a union."

"Good. That means she can definitely get the house. Good

wages, loans and all that stuff."

"How you know this stuff?"

"My dad's a big supporter of unions. Black people, civil rights, unions, abortion. You know what that is?"

"No." I tried to sound it out.

"Say, your mom's having a baby, only she doesn't want it."

"Okay."

"She goes to the abortion doctor and they fix it."

"How?"

"They stick a vacuum cleaner in her pussy and suck it out."

"Yuck. Why not just give it to somebody? Give it to an orphanage. That's what they're for."

"See, the whole point is to get rid of it before anybody can see she's pregnant."

"My mom wouldn't do that."

"I guess it's really for young chicks, you know, like Muriel, that get knocked up."

"Muriel have an abortion?"

"Probably."

"What they do with the sucked-out baby?"

"It's not really a baby yet, just a tiny thing, like a bug. They flush it down the toilet."

"No, my mom wouldn't do that," I said, thirsty. I wanted a beer. I wanted one of the mansion-owners' beers. Not a Schlitz or Colt 45. "Would your mom?"

"Yeah. My mom's a feminist. Your mom should have the

right if she wants to abort. My dad's a feminist, too. My dad's really something, you'll see when you meet him."

Why would Mom want the right to do such a thing? I thought about us kids—there could be more of us, someday, and I wouldn't want to know that my brother or sister got flushed down a toilet, although flushing Dudley down a toilet wouldn't have been a bad idea. What would Bikini Dad say? Did he care about Mom's rights? Did us kids have rights—the right not to be a servant to your dad? It would be so much better if my pretend dad were real—perfect in every way the dingy briefs-wearing one never could be.

Heavy stuff! Wanting to change the subject, I said "You drink beer?"

"Not officially. And not Schoeling."

He hauled at full throttle, peddling or coasting downhill while standing up. At first I anchored to the spoiler bar behind me, leaning to see around his butt. But as our speed increased, I gripped his waist to hold on tighter, my legs tucked back in grasshopper style. The wind flapped the bottom of his shirt up. Sweaty hair vanished into Fruit of the Loom underwear elastic over the studs on his stained Big Hank jeans. Oil, mud, arm stink, and Captain Crunch cereal swirled around me in tornadoes of smells. The banana seat was big enough for two. He didn't seem to realize this until we pulled onto the sidewalk. He plopped down, applying brakes, and leaning into me. His boney back put out heat like a furnace.

We turned in an opening between red-flowered hedges. We entered a driveway from behind. "Get off," he commanded, then jumped off the bike. He told me to wait. I could hear him rummaging inside the garage. I peeked around the corner and could see the left side of the backside of the house. It was big, but little compared to the brewer's house he hated so much. It was painted yellow and white and was peeling like old man's dandruff. I could see a shirtless, hairy man pacing back and forth in a second floor window, a cigarette burning between his lips. He spotted me. I ducked out of sight.

"Noah," the man shouted.

Noah either didn't hear him or pretended not to.

The man leaned outside the window. "Who's down there?"

"Dad, it's me," Noah finally answered.

But a few seconds later Noah's dad pushed through the back screen door. He angled around and looked our way. "Who's there?"

"Dad, it's me. I forgot something."

"Hi, me. You sound just like my son Noah. Did I see somebody else?"

"It's my friend Cliffy. My soul brother."

I was about to step out from the shadows, but Mr. Baumgarten came to me. He was very tall, with a thinned and pigeon-colored version of Noah's hair. It was on his naked chest, the hair raking upward from his trousers. Big squishy nipples poked through the hair, like little gummy candies hidden in Easter basket grass. He wasn't milky white like Noah, but the pale grey of a sunless sky. His face was clammy with sweat. His bright blue eyes were like bird eggs sitting atop a nest of dark, swollen skin. He blinked strangely and slowly and rhythmically, like he was on a cake timer.

"A pleasure to meet you, Cliffy. You live in the neighborhood."

"No, sir. In Finlater."

"In Finlater, huh?" he said, pronouncing it the same way I did. "Is it getting as bad over there as I hear?"

"Yes, sir."

I didn't think he wanted to hear that it wasn't, just as Mom could never believe anything good about Finlater, so I added, "Worse every day."

"If our government wasn't so corrupt or really cared about the welfare of the poor, people would be given enough to live on and there wouldn't be ghettos."

"Yes, sir."

"I have a good mind to sell our house, move over there, and shake things up. I could become a liaison to the city and get things moving. But you know, the problems are much bigger than just that. I should run for mayor—then I could really do something."

I didn't know what he was talking about. The blue eyes stayed on me—like the way animals' sometimes do, like they don't really see you, or don't know what to make of you. He then smiled and I felt even weirder. P-S-Y-C-H-O-T-I-C. I looked down and noticed his hands—they were mangled, with fingers missing, and the skin patched with what looked like baloney. Now I really didn't know what to say.

"You're welcome here anytime. Bring your folks, I'd like to meet 'em."

I expected him to ask about top-secret dad, and was relieved when Noah appeared, red-faced and sweaty. He threw his arm around his father.

"Cliffy, you're talking to the best dad on earth."

"Or the worst," Mr. Baumgarten said, never looking away from me.

"He's the best, Cliffy."

"I'm going to run for mayor," Mr. Baumgarten announced.

"You'd be great Dad," Noah petted his shoulder. "We've got to go. You know where's the old bicycle?"

"What do you say we sell our house and move over to Finlater?"

"Whatever you say, pops."

"Your mom said no to the Congo. Maybe she'll go for Finlater."

"Oooo-kay, anything you say. Now, how about Dean's old bike? You know where it is?"

"Where bicycles go when no one's looking. Perhaps for a ride!" Mr. Baumgarten gave his strange smile again, told me how much a pleasure it was to meet me, bumped my hand against his, and then left.

Noah seemed suddenly gloomy. He tossed his head back, bit

his lower lip and mumbled.

"Your dad's great," I said.

"Yeah, he is. He's just not himself right now." He turned away, but added: "Sometimes he's a little weird."

"I guess dads are, huh?"

Now was a chance to plant the seed that would grow into Bikini Dad. "We haven't heard from my dad since I was in third grade. My mom even said she didn't know if he was ever coming back."

"Wow. Soul brother, that's too bad. You freaked out?"

"No, I don't really remember him."

"Maybe your mom'll marry a better dad for you. Somebody like my dad—not like he is right now, but the way he usually is."

"Yeah, that would be cool," I said. "SB, you're the only person I ever talk to about him."

"That's what best friends are for," Noah said.

I agreed, rubbing my sweaty palms on my pants.

"It's good with your mom being in a union and all. . . Well, I'll ask my dad about the house later."

"And I'll ask my mom, too."

"Cool."

Noah was keen on showing me the house he wanted my family to move in. As he pedaled us away, I could see his dad pacing in the upstairs window again, with a burning cigarette in his lips, muttering to himself. He didn't seem to see us.

I told Noah earlier that I had to be home by two, or else. It was already 12:55. Noah was hell-bent, taking corners too fast and pumping frantically. My feet scraped the ground as the bike leaned recklessly, and I wondered what the hurry was all about. I soon realized why, when we began crawling up a steep hill. I looked behind me and saw a posse of mean-looking kids in front of a store, staring our way.

"Fuck dang," Noah spat. He swerved the bike sharply, and we nearly capsized.

"What's happening?" I shouted into his back.

"Nothing, just a wrong turn."

Then I heard: "Look, the Jew boy got his spook with him, too." One of the posse called out something to the others. Just then, four of them broke away from the group and pursued us on foot. A coke bottle whizzed by us and shattered against a parked car.

"Fuck you!" Noah screamed.

He turned up a driveway, slammed on breaks, and shouted "Get off!" We ran with the bike across several yards to the next block, to furious barking and doors flying open. Then we hopped onto the bike again, and Noah pumped us in a new direction, laughing all the while.

Seeing we were clear of them, he huffed, "That was fun. You like fighting?"

"Yeah, sure." My voice cracked. My stomach ached at the thought of my cast-iron-cookware muggers. Plus, in the one real fight I had, I was dragged around by my neck scarf. It was no fun. But being called a spook, though, deserved revenge.

"Next time we'll get 'em."

"The fuckers," I said.

Noah laughed. Peddling fast again, he told me that at school last year a teacher asked him about his Christmas and he said his family didn't celebrate the holiday, they were Jewish. He admitted it in front of the whole class. Ever since, kids called him kike, Christ killer, Jew boy, dirty Jew. "You get the picture. We've been living here since I started kindergarten, and nothing like that ever happened before. My mom says I should have kept my mouth shut, but why should I?"

"Yeah, why should you?"

"We used to get swastikas in our mailbox, and phone calls, and all kinds of crazy stuff. Somebody even tagged our front door with a pink triangle—that's what the Nazis used to do to some Jew men, women and kids before gassing them."

Was gassing worse than lynching? Maybe being a Jew was worse than being a Nigger.

He was riled up. "I'm not scared. My mom's grandparents and uncles and aunts died in the Holocaust, in the concentration camps in Buchenwald—that's in Germany. Fuck 'em."

All I could think of was Frau Crites, with her brownies from a German heaven that even Noah would forgive.

"That's atrocious. That's reprehensible. That's despicable. That's abom-in-able."

"SB, please stop it with all the syllables, the giant words, and spelling-out everything already."

"Sorry. I can't help it. I just do it."

"It's soooooo annoying. What you got to prove? SB, you cool by me."

And he was by me, too. Spelling big words ain't shit, I thought. He's right.

I'd forgotten about the house for sale. I noticed neighbors watching us from behind blinds or curtains. Noah waved and we stopped in a driveway leading to a lopsided-looking house. It was tall, narrow, and hard-bit looking in a drunken way, with a busted screen door and spokes missing from the porch railing. It seemed big enough that us kids might each get a room, the yard was nice in size, and it was at the edge of Elmwood. The thought of having to pass those thugs every day wasn't a good selling point.

"Ain't it great? Y'all can fix it up real good. Y'all could put up a basketball hoop and everything. Bet it's better than the ghetto, huh?"

"Where's your place?"

"That way," Noah pointed through the house. "Not far. Won't it be cool for us to live near each other? We could hang out every day."

"Yeah, SB, that would be terrific."

"Hey, you wanna steer?"

Somehow the afternoon had vanished and I was ten minutes away from punishment.

"I really got to get home."

"You can ride us up to the park. How's that?"

"Okay, great."

I leaned and pumped as hard as I could. Not having a bicycle to ride regularly, plus hauling Noah's 115 or so pounds, I pooped out quick. Five blocks away from where we started, I was ready to stop. My standing position lowered to a sitting one. He laughed. His boney thighs gripped me, and he clamped his feet down on top of my feet on the pedals. His hands locked onto handlebars, touching my hands, and we pedaled together. His heart beat in my back. His breathing pushing into my ribs and breath burning my ears. The Breck shampoo and the sweat and his dirt ganged up in my nose. "This is cool, ain't it?" he said. Beads of spit sprayed my ear, and I closed my eyes, blind as we road down that street.

"Yeah, it's cool," I said.

"Until you get a bike…"

We rode fast into the park, the sky a pinkish smear of sun and clouds above the lumpy treeline. We rode past kids on swing sets and teenagers smoking cigarettes on the basketball court. They ignored us, and we them. Noah stopped where the path descended into woods.

"End of the line, buddy."

I got off.

"Hey, look at you," he said, pointing at my privates.

"Me, too." He stood up.

We compared pup tents. His was bigger, but then he was bigger.

"You wanna milk it?"

"Huh?"

I had no skill at this. Too bad that spelling masturbation and ejaculation didn't come with cum. I always wanted a lesson, but somehow it seemed, well, embarrassing.

No one was around, but his eyes did a quick check. He unzipped his pants and pulled out his thing. The shock must have registered on my face, as I fast looked away. But then my eyes came to rest on the red fat wiener twitching with each slide of his hand.

"Pull yours out," he ordered.

I did as told.

"I've never seen a soul brother's dick before."

I quickly figured out that the reason erections weren't my obsession yet wasn't because the first time I pulled and yanked until the juice came out it hurt and felt good at the same time. It was because you needed another body. Noah said, "It's nice. It's like an Oscar Meyer"—and said it matter-of-factly, as if he were talking about a turtleneck or a Matchbox Mustang.

Dingalings were supposed to be played with and to be shared.

"Spit in my hand, and I'll spit in yours."

Gobs of saliva into each other's hand. I followed his every lead, and soon we were tearing our wieners up. Nearly keeling over, I yelped as cloudy liquid spurt to the ground. He roared like Tarzan. His dick-spit landed on my sneakers. I stared down at the spot, spelling in silence S-P-E-R-M-A-T-O-Z-O-A-N, and then made a quick promise to myself to stop the spelling. We both cracked up.

"Sorry about that, soul brother," he snorted, as we both stared down at the shiny splotch on my prized white Converse gym shoes. Before I could protest, he grazed the tip of his finger across his dick head, then put his finger in his mouth. He grazed it again, only this time he put his finger in my mouth. And I let him. It was weird tasting. Like something salty was put in by mistake, plus the flavor of dirt. And it looked like cleaning fluid. My sneakers seemed no worse.

"I owe you one," I said, and then ran home, thinking about our form of debt repayment.

FamIly nIGHT

Mom's fish and chips had tasted better. Scabs of burned cornmeal batter covered the catfish. The chips were tangled in wormy onions to please Dad. Her coleslaw was never right, compared to Grandma's, and mayonnaise flooded our shallow plates in white chalk water. The table settings were kind of messed up too, a fork here, a knife there. Her head was obviously elsewhere. Not that it bothered me since mine was too—in my and Noah's underwear.

I wouldn't have even noticed her cooking at all, but Dad was ticking off his complaints behind her back. Mom had called us down to dinner but then had disappeared. Dad told us that she went to a neighbor's—the "white chick's"—and would be right back. Dad wasn't just passing through with a piled-high plate, on his way back to his TV spot in their bedroom. No, he was standing at the sink mixing a pitcher of Kool-Aide. Surprise wasn't the word. His efforts in the kitchen never went beyond lifting a beer or a chicken wing from the refrigerator, or warming something up for himself. Making Kool-Aide must have given him just cause to complain outright against Mom's cooking.

"I don't know, boys, looks like I'mma need Alka-Seltzer after eating this shit. I love y'all's mom, now, but blindfolded I can cook better than her."

I chuckled. It seemed a harsh statement to me, especially since there was nothing ketchup couldn't fix. And lots of it. We upended and slapped the bottle until our plates bled. Dad joined the fray by ordering Corey to bring him hot sauce. "Your mom's gonna poison us," he jabbed again from his now seldom-used spot at the living room TV table, in front of Walter Cronkite and the Evening News.

Dad's health advisory inspired Corey. He shrieked, clutched at his neck, and lurched from the table, stumbling to the floor. Dad seemed to find this hilarious, for he let out a shout of laughter that ended in coughing spasms and a chewed-catfish spray. We couldn't be sure if he wasn't really choking to death on a fishbone, but the whole episode was funny enough that even mean Dudley snickered. After a long swig of beer, Dad said, "Damn, see what I mean. I'm going have to start eating out."

His Kool-Aide I admit was dynamite. I wondered if he harbored secret talents. I was a connoisseur of the liquid in the smiling glass picture. Mom often was stingy on sugar, to save money and our teeth, but the sour result left us kids bitter. Dad's black cherry looked perfect—no dune of sugar at the bottom, and with a rich, sweet color. I chugged down a glass so fast my head hurt. An aching stomped around my forehead, and when I shut my eyes I saw a square of yellow light. I wondered if I had a brain tumor like Reba in Days of Our Lives, Mom and Grandma's favorite soap opera. I wondered if I would die before I could tell Noah I was dying, before we milked our wieners again, before my fourteenth birthday, before we moved into the new Elmwood house.

Dudley and me traded tense looks. It wasn't about Dad's

knocking Mom's cooking, but about his afternoon plans versus mine. Dudley I believed had been rubbing up against this girl named Maybelline. The last few Saturdays, him and Santiago both had disappeared from our local playground for hours at a time, with a well-rehearsed alibi and a sworn-to-silence Corey tagging along. Now he was pissed. Before dinner, he sniped at me, "You think you're slick, huh? You're keeping Corey next week." Corey's open, silly eyes confessed that whatever Dudley had been up to wasn't a complete success. Corey maybe had had his own devilment, with girl-crazy Dudley clueless. Corey was wearing a bullet holster belt I'd never seen before, and I wondered why he said "that's for me to know, and you to find out" when I asked where he got it. A Mounds Almond Joy would bribe me some ammunition for future use, if necessary. But I really didn't care what they had been up to. My secrets were better.

We were done eating when Mom finally returned.

"I'm sorry," she said, a light film of sweat on her forehead. She seemed breathless. "I was at Connie's. She's sick. Female troubles."

I didn't know what female troubles were, but I knew bloodstained Kotex and a strange sickening smell were involved. Connie was our neighbor three courtyards away. She was white and about Mom's age, but not as pretty, with wheat colored hair and tropical fish-colored eyes. The father of her two little light brown girls with yellowish wiry hair was a black man killed in Vietnam. You could tell Mom both admired and pitied Connie. Connie had tossed aside a good Chicago family for love and paid a price for it. That's what Mom related to, I guessed, but it was like she couldn't quite believe it because only poor folks make such sorry choices. She once told me after a Connie visit: "She says she married a prince, a tragic prince. I guess even a good man can bring even the best woman down." Mom and Connie didn't seem to have much more in common than Finlater and young children. Connie read books and wordy magazines all the time, and her talk sounded smarter than Finlater, smart like a schoolteacher. She hadn't visited in a long time, since Dad's return, and I wondered if there wasn't a coincidence.

"Tasha got female problems, too?" Corey asked after the oldest of Connie's girls. Corey used to say he was going to marry Tasha.

"No, she's too young for Auntie Flow," Mom said. "Although these days girls are grown before eleven/twelve years old." Mom looked at Dad. Dad was into his TV, and paid her no mind until she lifted his bone-filled plate from the tray. "So how was the fish?"

"I ate it, didn't I?"

"Well, was it good?"

"Julia Childs, you ain't."

"You wouldn't want me to look like her."

"Who's that?" Corey said.

"Julia CHILD," I corrected, looking at Corey not dad, "is a white woman that cooks on TV."

"Honey child." Corey threw a hand to his boney hip.

Mom's sandals clicked on the grey-speckled linoleum floor, and she rolled her eyes away from our father toward us kids. "Boys, was your fish good?"

"It was great Mom," I said.

"Yep," seconded Corey, half-reaching for his throat.

Dudley looked toward Dad, then at me and finally at Mom. "The best, Mom. The best I ever tasted."

She petted Corey's head and winked at us.

"You boys up for a game of bingo tonight?"

"Bingo, wow, Mom, yeah, let's play," Corey cheered.

"Your father's going to play with us, isn't that right?" Mom didn't wait around for Dad's answer. "No one's stopping by, and we're not going anywhere. Tonight is family night. We can play Blackjack, Scrabble, or Monopoly or Life or Parcheesi, whatever you want."

"Bingo," Corey shouted.

"What about you, Dudley?"

"Blackjack."

"Cliffy?"

"Blackjack," I said.

"I'm with Corey," she said. "Cliff, it's two Bingos to two Blackjacks. Your vote decides."

I didn't take Dad for a Bingo man. I took him for a serious gambler. Our Blackjack stakes wouldn't be enough for him. We only played for nickels and dimes—chump change even to us kids. We played for higher stakes with each other and our friends, in the occasional game of dice.

Evidently Dad didn't hear Mom. "Cliff, what do you want to play?"

"Bingo, Daddy," Corey pleaded.

"Bingo."

Corey cheered while Dudley sulked. Dad yawned while Mom doted. Corey suddenly pounced on Dad, wrestling him on the couch. They rolled back and forth, with Corey laughing hysterically, his dark square feet kicking the air, and Dad bubbling "Lacey, what you put in that coleslaw?" Corey's seventy-five-pound body was airborne. Dad's big hands clutched him by the waist, dangled him mid-air. Corey's laugh was so high and loud it hurt my ears. Dad brought Corey down into his arms. Corey always liked being the center of attention, but he was Dad's favorite, that was clear as their faces seemed to melt into one. Whoever Dad was, Corey would be him as a man. Dudley must have had the same thought. He looked like he was suffering from a throbbing toothache. I think he was jealous of Corey's ease with our dad, like I was. I kicked Dudley lightly on the knee. Whatever it was he was thinking, I didn't want him ruining it for Mom. He ignored me, so I kicked him again. Then I noticed his watery eyes—filled with hunger and envy, like Frau Crites when she fed me brownies. He flicked the overflow away and chewed on a forkful of chips, but his whole self seemed tortured by Corey and Dad's fun. Guess he felt he had nothing to offer our dad except delivery service.

Mom's pleasure in watching seemed the match theirs in

playing. You could hear it in her giggles, in her "You two be careful," and in her breathing—light and pretty and full of anxious-sounding "ohs" and "nos" as Dad's TV table nearly tipped over. "Alright, you two," she warned, gushing. "That's enough." Their tussle finished with Corey draped over Dad's leg as lifeless as a coat.

"Cliffy, go get the Bingo set. You might as well get cards too."

I did as told, climbing the stairs two at a time. Family night needed my good news. The only problem was, how would I tell Mom without getting caught in a lie? Maybe I would wait until I won a bingo round, and then tell them as a by-the-way.

The bingo cards and chips were laid out, and banana pudding served. Pudding was Mom's specialty. It was box pudding she added bananas, cinnamon, vanilla wafers, whipped cream, and lately, coconut to. Nothing in the world that her hand touched tasted so good. We ate it practically every Saturday night, but I looked forward to it as if it were a holiday treat, and I sometimes loved it more than fried chicken legs. With or without Dad, making it seemed to make Mom happy. It was the one thing that was hers alone, and that she did that came out perfectly. All her meals were mostly bad imitations. It was Grandma Pleasant's fish and chips, Miss Glodine's fried chicken, Aunt Cora's pound cake, Grandma Douglas' sweet potatoes, macaroni and cheese, and so-and-so's whatever… perfect dishes all set for a Kodak moment and compliments. Of her banana pudding, even Dad said "… now you're talking, Lacey."

He was finishing off his first serving by the time I was seated at the table again, and waiting for seconds.

Mom decided to be the Bingo caller. She set up on the washing machine. Dad took her seat at the table, and replaced his pudding with a second Colt 45.

"You boys know this is an old lady game," he said.

"No it ain't," countered Corey. "You just saying that 'cause you're gonna get beat."

"Beat? We'll see about that."

"It used to be a bunch of old ladies playing at the Salvation Army, remember Corey?" I said.

"But at the rec center, all kinds play, even the country Niggers," Corey said.

"Corey!" Mom said.

Dad chuckled. "Country Niggers, huh?"

"Yep."

"Corey, I didn't raise you to talk like that."

"Like you don't call 'em country Niggers, Mom. You say it all the time."

"He's got you, Lacey. And ain't your people from the country? Mine are."

"He's got me nothing! And no, my people aren't from the country. My dad's people come from Memphis, my mom's from Louisville."

"Lacey, that's just what you know, but your people came by

way of the auction block and cotton fields just like the rest of the country Niggers, and city Niggers, too."

Mom glared at him. "Well, regardless of where they come from, we ain't like the trash around here. And I'm an adult, I can say anything I want. Corey isn't."

"That's what's called... what's the word..."

"Xenophobia," I said.

"Zena-a-what?" Dad said.

I repeated the word, watching Mom as I did.

"What does that mean?"

"Somebody who's afraid of foreigners. And I guess you could say the country blacks are foreigners."

"Well, I'll be," Dad said. "Where you learn big words like that, boy?"

"School, and on my own," I said, looking between Dudley, my mom and dad, waiting for Corey to humiliate me all over again.

"But he can't spell Fin—"

Mom cut Corey off, "I'm not afraid of the country people. I just don't like 'em."

Dad guzzled his beer while he appeared to think on what Mom said. Then he threw out: "And Tennessee is the South. And Kentucky too, last time I checked."

The tease and please in Mom's smile disappeared. "Corey, both your daddy's people and my people come from the South."

"Well, shit, Lacey, I guess that makes us southern Niggers,

and you could even say country Niggers, since you have to be southern to be country," Dad smirked.

"Shit, yeah," Corey said.

"That's it, no more cursing in this house. Cliff, these boys are impressionable." She took a deep breath, calmed her tone to a loud whisper. "Honey, you're supposed to set an example."

"Lacey, boys been cussing since Creation. You don't want a bunch of sissy boys. Long as they ain't cussing in school."

Mom's foot kicked the washing machine, and we boys snickered. Mom loved her late-model Kenmore washing machine, so it wasn't intentional, I was sure.

"Let's get this game going," Mom said. "Old ladies move faster than y'all."

"I'm ready," Corey shouted.

"Ready," Dudley followed.

"Been ready," Dad belched.

I nodded.

"First number, B6," Mom called. She sipped a beer, too.

Four rounds went smoothly, Corey winning two and Dad taking the others. Corey's gloating got worse with each hand. "Told you I was going to whip you," he said to Dad. To us he said, "What's wrong with y'all tonight. Dad, should we let them win a hand?" The taunts kept Dad interested. Whether Bingo was for old ladies or not, he crowed after each win, and retaliated against Corey with "Okay, boy, what you gonna do now?" He drooped back in his chair, leaning like he did behind the wheel of the Thunderbird, looking ever so Superfly. By the fifth round, though, the thrill was gone. He lit a cigarette, sending smoke rings into the air. My eyes soon burned, and Dudley coughed.

I was bored with Bingo and family night, mostly thanks to stupid Corey. It seemed to me that the moment to tell about the Elmwood house had passed and right now I didn't care. I'd rather splash in the tub with my memories of Noah. I was absent-mindedly laying chips on numbers Mom called out, not realizing that I was close to winning.

"H12...V2... S5..."

"Bingo," I shouted, nearly upturning the table.

"I gave you that." Corey stuck out his tongue.

Dudley hotly said, "I'm not playing any more Bingo. Let's play Scrabble."

"Why, it ain't like you a spelling bee champ like Cliffy," Corey cut.

"Sore loser," Dad said.

"I'm not a sore loser."

"You take it after me," Dad allowed.

Dudley seemed more, not less bothered, a razor sharpness in his eyes. "I don't take nothing after you."

Dad's lips smiled, but it wasn't out of fun. "Is that how it is, Dudley?"

Dudley said nothing back.

"Okay," Mom said. "Scrabble it is."

Corey turned to me and said, "Hey champ, can you spell

FIND-LATER?"

I realized that this was my chance, while we put away Bingo and started Scrabble, but I was so thrown off by Corey that I was confused.

"Me and Delrico... uh..."

"F-I-N-L-" Corey giggled.

"Me and Delrico..." I shouted over him, "...ran into a friend from school, and in Elmwood there's a really nice..."

The phone rang. Dad ejected from the table. Mom's eyes followed his body and froze there. Her concentration seemed focused on breaking the phone connection. It didn't work. Dad shook his head, said "Naw, I ain't doing nothing... That's a damn shame... I don't mind... Sure, let me throw some clothes on and I'll pick you up." Then he hung up.

"That was Red." Red was Dad's brother, so-called because he had red hair. "Red's stuck at a gas station over there in Erlanger. His car broke down. I'mma get him."

Mom's clenched face spoke all there was to say. What I saw was disapproving, pissed, even sad.

Corey begged, "I'll go with you, Daddy?"

At this Mom flinched. She looked at Dudley and me both, and I thought she was going to suggest we all go. If we did, there wouldn't be room in the car for Red.

"Corey, my boy," Dad said, "if it weren't almost past your bedtime I'd take you up on it."

Dad waited. Obviously Mom's permission wasn't required.

But something was. Some kind of acknowledgment that a brother was in need, and Dad was a brother indeed. Without choice.

Mom finally said, "Fine. Pick up some sausage at A&P on your way back."

"I can do that. I think I'm running low on beer, too."

Her eyes glassed over, following him across the room, but then she looked away. Her tight-boned hands fidgeted and wrung. I thought she was going to go after him, but she didn't. She tried to smile at us, yet was blind to us, staring at his empty chair.

The house. Tell her about the house, I thought. "Mom," I said, "...so what I was trying to tell you was there's a..."

"I see," she said. She suddenly stood up. Gravity seemed to be the only thing holding her to the ground. "Let's play," she said. Her arms stiffened as her hands anchored to the chair. Anger boiled up in me, over what I was unsure. We managed to play two hands of Blackjack, and then tears seeped from her eyes.

Dad threw a sharp outfit together, lickety-split. Lime green bellbottoms flapped as he strutted across the room, blowing Mom a "I'll see you later, baby" kiss and us a "that was fun, boys, we have to do it again, after Dudley gets an attitude adjustment" wave. Then out the door he went. Mom's interest and happiness chased him to destinations unknown.

"Boys, go to bed."

"But Mom..." Corey protested.

"Now."

Behind our door, Dudley said, "I hope he never comes back."

"I hope you shut up," Corey shouted.

Still steaming at Corey from earlier, I said, "How do you spell asshole, Corey, 'cause that's what you are."

"At least I know where I live."

We heard a crash downstairs, the sound of glass breaking. It shut us kids up. It took our words away. None of us went to investigate. We knew better. Loud shouting woke me up in the middle of the night, but it didn't last long. Soon after, their bed shaking meant all was fine.

She was in love.

pUssY wHIpPeD

Sundays normally were hell. Or just the church part of it, actually. It wasn't that I was afraid of God, or had anything against Him. It was just that having to be there for two to four hours made me cross, hateful, and blasphemous. Plus it seemed to me that the regulars, the good God-fearing folks, who didn't have diddly-squat, liked to pretend they had a lot to flaunt—whereas the ones that had a whole lot showed up on holidays and funerals, in fancy cars and dressed to kill, all made possible by money they didn't tithe away every week. That's where Sunday-based faith got you—broke and with a sore butt!

Even now that I might have done something that would send me to hell, I felt no need for church. From my point of view, the milking session with Noah and the lies I told were just boy things. Maybe the other reason I hated Sundays was because I couldn't wait for school on Monday. But that was all before I had an agenda. Now Sunday was a chance to bring up the Elmwood house. Plus I could question Father Ferdinand about Jews, him being a learned man. He would appreciate the attention since I usually shunned his. His fingers seemed to feel a need to pinch me on my already-sore and numb butt. His sentences were as overweight as he himself was, stuffed with big easy-to-spell words like "balderdash" and "poppycock." I figure maybe his exotic references like "Tahiti" and "Punjab"—might have something to do with Jews. I'd also see Grandpa Pleasant there, and then again later at dinner, and could seek his knowledge about Jews, too. You could count on Grandpa to deliver the bitter with the sweet. Grandpa had answers for everything, although Grandma sucked her teeth and made a "nonsense" flip of her hand at most things he said. If nothing else Father Ferdinand could confirm or deny Grandpa's observations. My ultimate authority would be the school librarian Mrs. Greenbacher. From her, maybe I'd learn so much about Jews that Noah's family would take me in after I ran away from mine. Or, soaked in knowledge, I'd just turn into a Jew.

Sunday breakfast usually was nice. Only there was no breakfast waiting for us that morning—the one and only Sunday in my life that I was actually excited about church! There was no Mom either. Us kids puzzled over what to do. Was Mom even home? I thought about Dad's saying we were grown enough that she could leave us at home alone at night.

But from the bathroom window, I noticed the Thunderbird in the parking lot, lit up in the sun like an idol for worship. Also, Dad's snores rumbled from underneath their bedroom door.

"Maybe she's bleeding again," Corey said.

"Men-stru-a-shun is every 30 days, doo-doo bird. She'd just had hers," I said.

"Ugh, what's that smell?"

"What…"

"You must be having yours, since you know so much about Aunty Flow and buying fancy panties."

"Shut up, Corey," Dudley barked. "Maybe he did something to her."

"Corey's right, Dudley, you're nuts," I said, suddenly sick of his doom and gloom about our dad. But I was afraid all the same. I leaped upstairs to knock on their door, but Mom came out just as I lifted my hand. The hall was dark.

"Cliffy, you scared me," she said, clutching her chest.

"Sorry, Mom. We were... We going to church this morning?"

"I'll be down in a minute."

I told my brothers she was on her way down. "Don't look like we going to church, though."

"Yippee," Corey cheered. "I don't know why we have to go all the way out there to get bored to death. I can't stand all those fat kissy old people with bad breath, and that stupid, snaggle-toothed deacon Rufus."

Dudley didn't look relieved, just angry, as usual.

Mom's footsteps on the stairs quieted us. She rounded the corner in her bathrobe, then stopped at the kitchen entrance, standing just outside the cone of light.

She said in a low voice, "I'm sorry to keep you waiting. Your mom's not feeling too good today." Her arms pretzeled over her chest, one palm cupping her cheek. She didn't look good either, but in my experience, without makeup all moms looked a little sickly.

I asked what's wrong.

"Female problems."

"But you had female problems two weeks ago," Dudley said.

"Other female problems. Dudley, why don't pour your brothers cereal for me."

He did not answer but did as told.

"And put the dishes in the sink when you're done and go outside and play. Only you better stay near home, and be here by two-thirty. We still might go to Grandpa's for dinner, and I don't want to have to go looking for you boys. And Cliffy, you've got Corey today."

"Oh, Mom." Corey stuck his tongue out at me.

"Oh, nothing, it's your turn. Actually, I want all you boys to stay together today."

Dudley gasped. "Mom, I'm not staying with them. I got something else to do."

"What you got to do, Dudley? You only just found out we're not going to church."

Dudley walked over to Mom, staring hard at her. She backed up, moving a little farther into the living room's shadows.

"Why you holding your face?" he demanded.

"Boy, that lip's gonna get you in trouble. You need to mind your business and do what you're told. But just so your head isn't all over the place, and not that it's any of your business, I've got a toothache. It kept me up all night, which is the other reason I'm not feeling so good." She then turned away and went toward the stairs. "Remember, two-thirty."

"Two-thirty," Corey said.

"Two-thirty," I seconded.

Dudley slammed three cereal bowls on the table.

"Dudley, you heard what she said about that lip," I said. "Cut it out."

"What tooth make you want to hide your face like that? Did you see her? She was trying to hide. Her face is all red. He did something to her."

"He gonna do something to you," Corey countered.

"Fuck him."

Maybe Mom was hung-over from drinking and didn't want to admit it. I guess a toothache could make a person look sick.

Mom made a quick reappearance, just as we were about to go out the back door, and her long hair was out and pulled to the side. "Two-thirty, don't be late," she said, smiling and holding her stomach.

I was now convinced Dudley just had it in for Dad. He was definitely becoming a teenage psycho. The combination of Dad, memories of him, and puberty was too much. I was thinking all kinds of reasons Dudley was going nuts, and then the little hole under his left shoulder made a flashbulb kind of connection in my brain. All us kids had funny kid scars, but only Dudley had anything like that. It was round like an eraser head and deep like a little well.

Outside in the courtyard, I said, "Dudley, can I ask you something?"

"Depends on what I get if I answer."

"Watcha want?"

The ridges on his forehead were like knuckles.

"I want for you two to leave me alone."

Corey for once was quiet.

"Okay, Dudley. I accept, but only if you answer. Promise?"

"Okay. Shoot your question."

"That scar on your shoulder. Dad do that to you?"

His mouth dropped and fingers spread open as if to hide something, or to show me he had all ten fingers.

"Who fucking told you that, huh? Who?"

"Nobody…"

Then he went berserk. He grabbed me by the throat and was choking me. Corey jumped on his back and we all tumbled to the ground.

Finally Dudley let me go and shoved Corey aside, hoisting himself up. "You fucking punks, both of you." Then he ran off.

"You're the punk," Corey shrieked. "Pumpkin head punk motherfucker, and your girl's a douche bag dog face bitch."

I clutched my throat, shocked that Dudley could have, and wanted to, hurt me.

"I can't stand him. Just because he don't like having a daddy don't mean he can go off willy-nilly attacking us, or try to spoil it for the rest of us. Why don't he go away? Nobody'll miss him, the creep. He just jealous Dad never gives him nothing."

"Corey, he got his reasons," I said. Was it a cigarette burn? Or had he been stabbed with something, a pencil, a knife?

"They ain't reasons, he's just crazy. He got that girl's pootang and now he acting like he somebody. He's a nobody."

"Whatcha talking about?"

"Maybelline, that girl he and Santiago go see, she let Dudley stick his dick in. Santiago stick his in, too. I saw 'em do it."

"What?"

"She let me, too."

"What dick you got?"

"I got one, and it's bigger than yours, too."

"You did it to her?"

"Did it."

"You lie like a rug."

"What you want to bet?" he said.

"A dollar."

"That's how much it cost for her to put it in her mouth. She let us do it to her for two dollars so she can get her some new clothes. He goes over there every day. He's pussy-whipped."

"Liar."

"I'll prove it to you."

"How?"

"We'll go over there."

"Now?"

"Her Mama leave her and her sisters alone all the time."

"Wow, all the time?"

"Ain't never there, they ain't seen her stank butt in over a month. They don't go to school or nothing, just selling pootang for two bucks."

All I could think to say was "Where Dudley get two bucks?"

Corey laughed like I was the dumbest person in the world.

"He stealing it," Corey said.

"Stealing it? Who from?"

"Who you think?"

"I don't know."

"Dad."

"Dad?"

"Yep."

Dudley, a psycho thief? My own quick-change to cum-licker-masturbator was nothing compared to Dudley's sins. I couldn't believe my ears. Not just that Corey knew these things, and had vocabulary I'd never heard him use before, but that he put his wiener in a girl. Or that a girl would let him. I could barely believe that Dudley had been tortured and was doing girls at fifteen—it definitely explained why he was so nuts all the time. But Corey! What kind of a girl lets an eleven-year-old boy do that? I was stone-cold jealous.

We ran to south Finlater, toward what I figured would be a real twilight zone. The Twilight Zone was my favorite program on TV. Things weren't what you thought they were. People who claimed "to want to serve man" really wanted to cook you up as Sunday dinner. If Corey was right, Dudley was just fronting with his dad hatred to steal from him. And what was Corey's source for money? Grandma always said "What's the world coming to?" when a thing makes no sense.

The ho Maybelline and her sisters lived on Compton Court, in the deep south of Finlater. Here lived all the "trifling, just-this-side-of-slavery Niggers" of Mom's fears. Even the bus avoided it, turning left and speeding in the opposite direction. Our part of Finlater was nice and clean, even if it all looked alike, but I couldn't understand why theirs was so nasty—like they didn't want it to stay clean. The dogwood blossoms and red azalea flowers and perfume smells filled all Finlater. But here the courtyards were bald and diseased-looking. Broken down cars were all over the parking lot like forgotten corpses from a long-ago battle. Obnoxious graffiti—most misspelled—tagged all the buildings with BITCHS, MUTHAFUCKERS, THE MANS, THE PIGGS. Running through the woods to school at night couldn't be as dangerous as it seemed here. Corey didn't look as scared as I felt, but he didn't act at ease, either.

"We gonna get jumped," I said.

"Naw, we won't. I got my knife, don't worry."

"Knife?" Now I knew we were going to get killed. "I'm going back."

"We're almost there. Maybelline lives right past that building."

Just as we got near the building in question, who should we see but Dudley. He must have just arrived. Maybelline, who I guessed was sixteen, was pushing the door open. They disappeared inside.

"See," Corey said, stopping and pointing.

"That don't mean nothing."

"Come on," he shouted, running again.

"I'm not going in there."

"Come ON."

"We're going get in trouble."

"You're such a puss-eeee."

Corey gave me the flip as he ran toward the door.

I just knew killers, gangs, thieves, thugs, drunks, and addicts were scoping me out. I spun around to see which direction to run in, then tore off after Corey. He cackled as he knocked on the door. In his best Tin Man voice, he said, "Maybe the Wizard will have some spare courage for you, cowardly lion."

"Maybe you'll get a brain."

It wasn't Maybelline who answered the door, but a big titty girl in a polka-dot swim top with thick nappy black hair pulled into puffs like wild earmuffs. Her bracelets clattered, and her earrings looked like Slinky loops.

"What y'all want?"

"Maybelline." Corey said her name the way Mickey Spillane would, like he would start beating people if anybody stood between him and what he came there for.

"May, girl, you got more company."

"Who dat?"

The big girl looked down at us. "You Dudley's brothers?"

"Yeah, that's right," Corey's eyes switched back and forth between me, her and the sliver of room we could see beyond the backdoor.

"Y'all favor, I can tell. You got some money?" she was

looking at me when she said it.

I shook my head no.

"This ain't no lay-away, boy."

"I got money," Corey said.

Looking at me again, she said, "Got a little sugar in your blood, I can tell."

"Huh?"

"Sweet boy," she winked, licking oily lips. Her gums were as dark as a chocolate bar.

"Thanks," I said.

She said "sweet boy" again, as if making a diagnosis like tooth decay or flat feet. I was embarrassed. I didn't know if I was being insulted or complimented.

"I'm a sweet boy, too." Corey's lip hung with jealously, neglect, rejection.

Her laughter jiggled her titties. "Don't worry. Mama's gonna give you some, when you a little older and your thang don't feel like a pin prick."

She let us in. We went through a yellow kitchen with doily curtains, Corey leading the way. The big girl was in grimy slippers, and her crusty feet dragged and her butt wobbled to the stove, where she was frying bacon. A kite of smoke curled over the kitchen. "Hope y'all ate already," she said. "This ain't Frisch's."

Dudley was sitting on the sofa watching cartoons. His eyes full of threat.

"Mom said we should stick together today," Corey said.

"I'm going to take you out." Dudley seethed.

"Where's Maybelline?"

"She went upstairs."

Dudley's look softened as Bugs Bunny stuck his fingers into Elmer Fudd's rifle.

"Who's that big girl?" I whispered to Corey.

"That's Chanel, Maybelline's big sister. She's eighteen. Her pootang cost ten bucks."

I was more interested in Chanel than in Bugs Bunny. I could see half her body from where I sat on the sofa. A black bare leg shiny with Vaseline, the outward curve of her wide hips and thick butt pushing against loose pink hotpants. Marvin Gaye whined on the radio. Chanel grooved her hips against the sink cupboard, bending over to show what she was charging $10 for. A wet stain boiled on the sling of her hotpants, and flesh that looked like dark chicken gristle escaped the pink confines. "Yuck," I said, and my stomach churned. Shortly, she clattered and wobbled through the room with her bacon sandwich, winking at us as she passed. "You boys can't be ganging up in here like this. It's Sunday, so we gone make a 'ception today. I got friends coming by in a hour."

Dudley looked sick. A glass of purple liquid was on the end table in front of him. "Y'all better go," he snarled at us when she was out of sight, then lifted the glass.

"I ain't going nowhere. Sugar boy there can go," Corey giggled. "Give me some of that wine."

Wine? I stared at Dudley's glass. "I'm leaving." I had wanted to see Maybelline, but now I didn't care. I wanted to get away from them.

"Good," they both said at once.

"And you owe me two smackaroos," Corey added.

I slipped out the front door and ran farther south to avoid trouble, and then all the way to Winneste Avenue, the road that linked all Finlater, top to bottom. I figured that if anything happened to me somebody would see it. The sunny morning had faded into a grey afternoon, and the sky rumbled with distant thunder. So I ran faster. Finlater was built on a long sloping hill. The road running through it wasn't at all straight. The tires of cars speeding southward screamed on the sharp curves. I was steadily watching these cars, all prepared to lunge for my life, when I saw the familiar Thunderbird, Dad behind the wheel. A woman was on his left, but it wasn't Mom. It couldn't be Mom—Mom would never leave us without word of where she was going. Dad's and my eyes met as the Thunderbird shrieked on the curve and sped out of sight.

Mom was at home. She was all prettied up with makeup, more than I ever remembered her wearing. She was prettier than Dianna Carroll.

"Too bad you boys didn't get here a little sooner, we could have gotten a ride to the bus stop. Your father just left. Where're your brothers?"

"They're coming. Yeah, I saw Dad." I was going to ask about the lady in the car, but thinking of Dudley's crazy talk and the fear it inspired, I didn't.

"Good. I told Grandpa and Grandma we'd be there by three."

"You feeling better, Mom?"

"Yes, honey, I feel much better." She kissed my forehead. "Mom feels wonderful. I hope you didn't rack up a bunch of sins today."

"No, I didn't..."

"Oh, before I forget, a boy named Noah called." She pulled a piece of paper from the telephone pad. "Here's the number."

I stared at it as if it could speak.

"Who's that?"

"A friend from school. I've told you about Noah before."

"My brain, these days nothing stays in it. I'm glad you're home because I wanted to talk to you without your brothers around. You're much more mature than they are, much wiser I think. You know, sometimes, Cliffy, things happen that you don't mean to happen. Sometimes you might do something that you didn't mean, and you know it's wrong and you'll never do it again. You understand?"

"No."

"Sometimes we say things or do things that we regret because we know it's wrong. You know, Dudley has made me so mad I've hit him, but I didn't mean to do it. Anger just took control of me. Lord knows you boys—not you, sweetie—need the belt sometimes, but punishment is different than just hitting somebody. You understand?"

"Yeah." I thought about Dudley. "Is that why Dudley has that mark on his shoulder?"

Mom's expression changed, and she looked away. "Well, you know, it was an accident. Your father did that to Dudley when he was a little boy. He had Dudley across his knees and a lit cigarette fell from his mouth and… It was an accident."

"Okay."

"Why you bring that up?"

"I was just wondering."

"Well," she said, looking away from me. "That's not what I was talking about. I wasn't home when it happened, but anyway it was an accident."

"Guess you shouldn't smoke and hold a baby at the same time."

"That's right…"

Whatever Mom had intended to say got dropped. She leaned down so our eyes met. At first I was afraid of what she might see. We were now strangers in a way. But I loved to lie in her arms and missed the feel of her kisses. Just then, she planted one upon my cheek and pulled me into her body. The crooked world seemed straight again.

"I love you, my Cliffy."

"Love you too, Mom."

"If you brothers aren't here in five minutes, I won't be loving them so much. Where were you anyway?"

"At a friend of Dudley's. Can I call Noah?"

"Okay. But keep it short. And we won't tell your brothers, will we? We can't have you boys on the phone all day and night." She glanced at her watch. "You got five minutes, or until your brothers come home, whichever comes first."

Mr. Baumgarten answered. He breathed hard into the phone. Noah wasn't home. "It's Cliffy, Mr. Baumgarten. Remember, I met you last…"

He hung up. He might be a terrific dad, but he sure was nuts.

Mom looked annoyed that Corey and Dudley showed up a half hour later, both grinning from ear to ear. "Dudley, how do I look?" She positioned herself in front of him.

Us kids admired how beautiful our mother was still, but the question was Dudley's to answer. "You look pretty, Mom. Real pretty. The prettiest mom in Finlater."

"Thanks." She went to kiss him, and he, caught off guard, stiffened, but soon melted as her arms locked around him.

"Boys, we're going to Grandpa's. Y'all wash up."

"Mom, it's gonna storm," Corey said.

A crack of lightning backed him up.

"I know. We're taking a cab. Your dad gave me some extra money. Wasn't that nice?"

"He's the best," Corey said.

Mom's eyes beamed gold at praise like that. "It's so good when all my young handsome men are home. My fine young men."

EARLY BIRDS AND WORMS

There was so much to tell Noah I couldn't sleep. I jumped out of bed on the tail of Mom's 5:30 A.M. departure. I dressed quickly, shook Dudley awake, and told him I was going to school. I didn't care if he heard me or not. Knowledge of my brothers' lives on the sly meant I could do whatever I wanted.

I gobbled cereal down and left the empty bowl. It was 6 A.M. when I slipped outside into May 12th's morning cold. Our little part of Finlater sparkled with newness from the thunderstorm. The buildings, the streets, the bushes, and even the air had been put through God's loud carwash.

I ran through Finlater toward the path to school. Twigs became branches and sewers small dams unable to drain. The baseball field had flooded over, its glassy surface reflecting a bright dancing sky. The woods had taken a savage beating, with tree limbs scattered along the school trail. A huge tree I never noticed before had snapped apart, its top lying face down from the fatal blow, the branches bunched together and spread open like helpless arms. A mist still hung in the air as if from a giant plant sprayer, and the sun glittered above the canopy of trees. Tolkien's hobbits, dwarves, elves, giants, fairies, and unicorns must live in such woods, I thought, unafraid.

Puddles were for splashing. By the time I arrived at Noah's, my sneakers were soaked and so were my jeans from the knee down. Morning dew and sweat trickled down my face. I stared at the house, trying to insert myself into Noah's brain. Where inside the house was he? I followed the tar driveway around back, and I could hear the Baumgartens at breakfast. They sounded like one varying voice, like birds chirping. What were they talking about? Maybe a trip to some fun place where kids ride rollercoasters, eat candy bars and peanut brittle and win stuffed animals all day. Coney Island. Disney Land. What were they eating? Coffee cake with icing and hot chocolate with whipped cream in it—that sounded like something white people with big houses ate for breakfast. Or maybe waffles with chocolate sauce, or even Eggs Benedict (whatever that was). Maybe Jews were different. Maybe they ate whatever they wanted, each something different. Maybe everybody had their own refrigerator stocked with all their favorite foods. What was Noah eating? Was he even there? Was he thinking of me? Sleepless like me? Maybe he'd had the same thought about seeing me, and maybe he'd gone to the park to intercept me on my way to school. What if he hadn't? What if his phone call had been to give me an ultimatum—either your hero daddy gets clothes at Ben's or else? Or maybe he just didn't want to be friends.

Just like that, my excitement shriveled into a kind of terror that I shouldn't have come. That I'd be sent away by my best friend in the world. I'd get lost in Elmwood, eventually wandering into a block of thugs. I'd be tied up and beaten and castrated in some basement, never to see my sweet mother and obscene brothers again. I was about to run when low barking came—sounding more like a deep cough. The backdoor suddenly flung open. A huge black dog bounced through, lunging off the porch steps, with a big hapless grin on its dopey face. It lumbered straight toward me, barking not with threat but like it wanted to play. It seemed like a small hairy horse to me. I froze in place because that's what you're supposed to do when a dog comes at you. It made a grumbling sound, and the little slits it had for eyes seemed to be laughing at me, a string of slobber swinging from its flabby jaws. It sniffed around my jeans and sneakers, its tail making figure eights, until more interesting smells lured it away. I watched it bounce across the yard, where it disappeared behind bushes. I looked up and noticed the Baumgartens watching me through the window.

A short, wiry woman came out on the porch, "Cupcake, you stay out of the Krasdale's yard, you hear me?" Then to me she said, "Well, look at you. Can I help you?"

"Ma'am, I'm here for Noah. Is he still home?"

"He's upstairs getting ready for school. You can come in if you want. We're as harmless as Cupcake. I'm Noah's mother."

Chapped lips smiled at me. She was pinkish and her cheeks looked smeared with strawberry jam. Inside, she asked for my name, then announced into a little electronic box mounted on the wall, "Noah, your friend Cliffy's here." Still smiling, she shoved crazy brown hair out of the way, then went back to the other children and her cereal bowl. It was a big kitchen crowded with stuff—a blender, a mixer, a toaster, a toaster oven, a mountain of dirty dishes in the sink. The table the kids sat at sprawled in old grainy wood. The refrigerator door doubled as a gallery for kids' drawings, announcements, silly Polaroids, postcards, all held in place by plastic fruit magnets.

"This is Leeza and Isaac."

Leeza, a freckly thing, gave a bothered hi. Noah had introduced us on the playground. Crazy hair must run in the family. Hers was like a rug rolled up and tied down with ribbon. The boy at the table had the weirdest hair of all, like chocolate cake frosting. He jammed a spoon in his cereal bowl.

"You're a friend from school?"

"Yes, ma'am," I said. "I've seen you drop Noah and Leeza off."

"Oh," Mrs. Baumgarten said. "Only if they're running late. They usually walk. Where do you live?"

"Finlater."

"Findlater, really." She pronounced the "d," but not as in "find" but silently, which made me feel a little better. This seemed correct—or at least closer to what I knew.

"I used to volunteer at a women's shelter there. It was mostly a place for battered women to turn to."

"I'm sorry ma'am, what's battered?"

"Violence against women, usually by men."

"Probably lots of women like that in Finlater."

"I remember all too well. But it's everywhere, really."

"We're looking to move. We're looking for a house in a nice neighborhood like Elmwood."

"Nice isn't the word that immediately comes to mind for this neighborhood."

I didn't understand and was going to ask what she meant,

but Noah came in just then, reddened and damp from showering, his wet hair slicked down and straight as straw.

"Hey Cliffy, whatcha doing here?"

"I thought maybe we could walk to school together."

"Great."

"Cliffy, would you like a muffin and juice?"

"Yes, ma'am."

"So polite and well-spoken, your mother obviously taught you manners," she said.

Isaac shouted at Leeza to move over and stop kicking him.

"Isaac has been taught manners, although you wouldn't know it." Mrs. Baumgarten's smile showed teeth that were grey and crooked. She served me a banana muffin and orange juice. Her kindly eyes were the color of prunes, the skin around them darkened and puffy. Her hands slipped quickly into her apron. I thanked her, and swallowed a bite of muffin and said it was "spectacular."

"High praise, indeed. Kids, please take notes on how to show gratitude and appreciation. Thank you, Cliffy. You probably don't have the distinction of being the first black boy to walk the morally corrupt streets of Elmwood, but you definitely do have the distinction of being the first to come by here. You're welcome any time."

I thanked her again. Noah toed my knee under the table, then jabbed his finger into my side.

"Boys, not at the table. Remember the fourth commandment:

THOU SHALT NOT HORSEPLAY." Then, "Cliffy, you're very brave to wander all the way here from Finlater. That's a long way for a young kid to be walking alone."

"Yes ma'am, but I'm used to it. Us kids all walk to school."

"Mom, I took Cliffy to see the house for sale over on Gardenia."

"Oy, wouldn't that shake things up around here."

I grinned with worthiness.

"What does your mom do?"

"She's a packer at the Brachs Candy factory. She works really hard."

"Interesting. You look like you could be the son of a woman I..."

"Huh?"

"Oh nothing." She cleared her throat. Seemed like she was going to say something else but changed her mind. Instead she said, "That sounds like a pretty stable job, But that house would never be shown to blacks... Cliffy, which is correct, blacks or negroes?"

"Doesn't matter none to me."

"Guess if I'm white, you're black. Except you're not black, you're beige. And I'm not white, I'm pink. It's all so silly, really." She shook her head, and I knew where Noah got his black/white thoughts from. "I'll look into the house. I could set up an appointment and bring your mom along. Maybe a lawsuit should be filed."

"See Cliffy, I told you my mom would help," Noah said. "Mom, Cliffy's mom doesn't need his dad to get a house, huh?"

"That depends."

"Cliffy's dad is a scientist in Arizona, like Oppenheimer."

"I see," Mrs. Baumgarten said. "I'll do what I can. Noah's father and I love a good cause," she added. Then, to Noah, "Is Dad up yet?"

Noah shook his head no. Mrs. Baumgarten's eyes blinked away, focusing on her yellow coffee mug. "Isaac, don't forget your milk money, and it's Hebrew class tonight, remember. And Noah, everybody's supposed to be home at four sharp, and that includes you."

"I don't know why we have to go," Leeza whined. "It's so boring."

"Of course it is," Mrs. Baumgarten said. "Four sharp."

"What's the point?"

"The point is it's part of your culture, and that's important."

"It's really jive, Mom," Noah said.

"We've had this discussion before, and you're not going to win here, kids, so forget it."

"Aren't you going to say, we'll thank you someday?" Leeza lobed. "I'll never thank you. Ever."

"Be glad you ain't a Jew, Cliffy," Noah smirked.

A striped, cross-eyed cat wandered in, meowed and rubbed against the stove. Mrs. Baumgarten poured multicolored kitty food for it, then added golden apples to lunch pails.

Noah ran upstairs, and Leeza and Isaac put on their galoshes while Mrs. Baumgarten quizzed Leeza on spelling. Leeza stumbled through "gastronomy" and Mrs. Baumgarten asked me if I knew. Of course I spelled it correctly and Leeza stuck out her tongue. Had she not, I might have shared my colossal bee failure. Mrs. Baumgarten lectured her on graciousness. Leeza rolled her eyes, hissed "bitch" from between her hamster-like teeth, and I was amazed that she wasn't smacked into tomorrow. Even deranged Dudley would never curse at our mom to her face.

As we were going out the door, she said, "Cliffy, I'll get your number from Noah and call your mom."

"Yes ma'am." Oh, boy. I wanted to say I should talk to my mom first, but I didn't. "My mom works all the time, and it's best to catch her on the weekends."

"Then that's when I'll call. Leeza, remember to bring your thermos home. Noah, make sure she brings it."

"How am I going to do that?"

Cupcake sniffed at a dead crow in the driveway, its claws facing heavenward and a worm sticking out its beak—the likely culprit in the bird's death. Leeza saw it and began to cry on the spot. Mrs. Baumgarten shouted from the porch, "What's wrong?"

"It's dead. It's dead."

The suddenly helpless Leeza allowed herself to be hugged by the "bitch," balling like a baby. "We'll just say a little Kaddish for it, and then we'll bury it in the backyard. Okay, honey."

"Mom, we have to go," Noah whined. To me he said, "Girls

are so stupid."

Mrs. Baumgarten looked at me. "All right, but close your eyes, boys, and reflect on the passing of life."

"So jive," Noah hissed. His mother spoke words in what I learned was Hebrew. She then sang a few bars of something sad. I looked up to the second floor window. A haggard, bearded, shirtless Mr. Baumgarten stared down at us. He looked like an old confused man. I waved to him, but he didn't wave back, like he didn't see me.

Just then, Noah looked up too, and grabbed my arm. "Mom, can we go now?"

"Only because Cliffy's here, and it's unfair to make him late, too."

Noah ran, and I ran after him. Just as we were neck and neck, he ran faster. I quickly showed him who was the better runner. I turned to glance at him and then pulled ahead. He was red-faced and puffing hard, with strands of still-wet hair stuck to his face. I banked onto a small grassy hill to pass other kids and jumped over small branches snapped off by last night's storm. I slowed down, and Noah ran past me as we crossed a street. It was like he didn't see me or the other kids, some shouting his name, or notice the car traffic at all. I could overtake him, I knew, but I didn't. I lagged close behind, enough to see Big Yank on his jeans back pocket and the light bouncing off their brass studs. As we turned onto our school's street, the energy left him. He coasted to a stop and swiped at his face, breathless and dripping sweat. He looked pained and beat, and yet like he wanted to go on.

"Okay, you won." I swiped at my forehead, only there was little sweat. I bent over to catch my breath. I added, "You're really fast."

"I wanna go to Mexico, to Tijuana. That's where I want to go." He wheezed and beat his chest with his fist, staring at the bright sky.

"You planning on running there?"

"Maybe."

"I'll race you."

His eyes were red and angry. "We can get us a one-way ticket. I'm never coming back here."

"Me either."

"Cliffy," I heard Corey's voice shouting. Corey, Dudley and the usual gang were coming out of the park—Delrico too, a heavy bag slung across his back. Corey and Delrico separated from the group, running over to us.

"Wow, you been out all night?" Corey seemed in awe of me.

"Yeah," I lied.

"I'mma tell."

"I'm sure Mom will love hearing about you drinking wine at Maybelline's."

Delrico and Noah stared at each other like two curs ready to tear each other to pieces.

Delrico said, "Corey thought somebody kidnapped you."

"No, still here."

Noah suddenly bolted off again. I ran after him. And that challenged Corey and Delrico to run after me. Which somehow seemed to tease other boys to join in. Before we knew it at least twenty of us were running down the middle of the shiny street, shouting and laughing. Car horns and the crossing guard's whistle shrieked angrily. There were no rules or dangers or a need to hold back. We were as free as I'd ever felt in my life, with not a thought about anything but running. My eyes were on Noah's hair flopping in the wind. It wasn't until other boys passed him that he seemed aware of what was going on. He turned back to look at me and all the boys running behind us. A grin erasing everything that came before that moment seemed to make him happy again. He shouted, "hot damn, hot damn!"

A Darky's Best Friend

History was last period. It wasn't my favorite subject. Bald, doughy Mr. Coursey loved to hear his own voice. Since us kids could never speak like his beloved Elizabethans, we had to listen. Except to criticize and tax our reading skills, he mostly ignored us. First day of school he told us he taught college a lifetime ago. No way did we believe he loved to teach us Elmwood eighth graders more. Most times he seemed to dislike us with a passion equal to his love of Shakespeare. Sometimes he'd glide into a poetry recitation, often from the Bard, which made his turkey goiter wobble. We'd watch him, snickering under our breaths. He was as round as a bell clapper but had a small pigeon face, with wisps of hair above his ears. His weight somehow balanced on small dainty feet, and he wore pilgrim's shoes in patent leather. We wondered if he had ever seen his shoes. His vision was so bad, his eyes were like specks of pale blue light at the end of a glass tube.

But his hearing was sharp, and our low whispers and giggles also set the turkey goiter wobbling.

"The Fall of Constantinople is of far more consequence than your Green Hornet comics swap," he might jab us.

Or "Ms. Schumacher and Ms. Patchel, stop your private nattering. We are building pyramids with the Pharaohs."

He tolerated having us kids read while he made foot patrol with what he called "the collection box." Every Christmas he donated his take to Goodwill or to an orphanage, or so he told us.

It took the entire school year and potato famines, pestilences, assassinations, deaths, wars, and conquests to make it to the American Civil War. Noah and I were far from slavery, the cotton gin and Emancipation Proclamation, and even from the Elmwood house, the wild race to school, dead crows, Hebrew lessons, our mothers meeting. We were writing notes about all the things we'd do in Mexico. I knew nothing about Mexico, and wished Mr. Coursey could redirect his lesson plan to Central America. One note Noah wrote said we'd eat tacos and burritos, and my note to him asked what those things were. He mimicked like he was chewing.

"Was Tonto Mexican?" I whispered.

"No, Indian."

"Who's Mexican?"

Mr. Coursey's voice sounded like canon fire: "Presidents George Washington and Abraham Lincoln would perhaps be overjoyed by the miscengenic friendship of misters Baumgarten and Douglas. Anybody know what mis-cen-gen-a-tion is? Nobody? Look at them."

His frankfurter-thick finger pointed at us. All eyes stared.

"Misters Baumgarten and Douglas, this lesson should be of particular interest to you. Do you know why?"

Noah and I glanced at each other.

"Mr. Baumgarten, do you know why?"

"No."

"And you, Mr. Douglas, do you know why?"

"No, sir."

"The Civil War was fought so you two could be friends. Well, it was fought for other reasons, but I daresay your friendship in this school right now is the benefit."

"But we didn't have anything do to with it," protested Noah.

"Mr. Douglas, do you know what I'm talking about?"

"Slavery."

"Yes, but more specifically. What about slavery?"

I stared at my desk as if there I'd find answers, but all I could do was sound the word out, breaking it into syllables that rolled silently off my tongue. Exactly what I did at the citywide bee, only I was wrong. Exactly what I felt then, only now I was hit by a sudden pounding headache and somersaulting stomach. Mr. Coursey's voice sounded like the announcer's at the bee. I had been feeling sick the moment we lined up on stage, when I looked out and saw all the kids and parents in the audience, an audience entirely of white people, the floodlights making everything look like a Martian spacecraft landing, only I was the alien creature, a word-loving Nigger boy from the Finlater projects. At our local school bee, I saw my brothers and classmates in the audience and wasn't afraid. Now I was alone—I couldn't even spot Principal Schor's face—and terrified. The announcer's voice and the audience's murmurs, sighs, gasps and applause were outside me, and I was not in my head, but floating around myself. I could still see the words that I spelled that afternoon, but I couldn't hear myself spelling them. I had done fine, terrific really—I could hear the audience cheering—until the announcer said all the new words were local color, many of them German in origin—neighborhoods, streets, foods. Oh, poop, I panicked. I wasn't prepared, but I didn't want to be eliminated. I just wanted to get off the stage. And then my turn came. The announcer said, "Find-lata." I asked him to repeat, feeling I was going to piss my pants. "Find-lata." Through my shaking voice, I asked what or where it was. "It's a neighborhood not far from here, in the eastern part of the city." I felt either sweat or pee or something wetting me, because I didn't hear the word in a way that I understood. That's when I really panicked. If I had kept my cool and just listened and not minded the wetness I felt in my underwear, I would have gotten it right, I knew, and yet…

"Mr. Douglas," Mr. Coursey said, "We're waiting."

"Miscengenic. M-I-S-C-E-N-G-E-N-I-C. Miscengenic."

"Bravo, Mr. Douglas. But spelling isn't the same thing as knowing. And we have moved on."

"Anybody know?"

No one did.

"Mr. Douglas wouldn't be permitted in this room, much less a friendship with Mr. Baumgarten. Class, what else would Mr. Douglas the slave not have been permitted to do?"

On and on he went. It rarely happened that the class went along with him, but it did, happy to participate in my enslavement, it seemed to me.

"Mr. Douglas, are you worthy of your manumission from bondage?"

Again I couldn't think fast enough.

"If you had read your lessons you'd know that word."

"I read the lesson. Manumission. It means freedom," I coughed out.

"Very good, Mr. Douglas." His lips opened to moldy teeth.

"And yet you don't pay attention to this of all lessons. And you persist in behaving like an ignorant darky—class, that's one of many unfortunately names the negro people were called."

Now anger came. It wasn't the same as the panic feeling. My skin burned and itched as I felt myself wanting to shout at Mr. Coursey to shut his mouth.

"Presidents Washington and Lincoln, then Roosevelt and now Truman, Eisenhower and the late Kennedy were your peoples' best friends. Do not disappoint the presidents and the people who set you free. The burden of history rests on your shoulders."

I nodded as tears dripped and splashed on the desk.

"Mr. Douglas, see me after class, please."

His was our last class. I couldn't look at Noah. I heard him hiss "that dandruffy fat creep" under his breath.

Class dragged the last twenty-minutes. I thought of all the things I had heard about slavery. Grandpa Pleasant told me that his grandmother, Lullabelle Mathias, was born a slave, at the time of the Civil War. At 109 years old she still lived on a patch of land in middle Georgia with "big man hands from working like a mule." So many things I could have said, but could not say. What was Mr. Coursey going to say to me? What would he do to me? Why was he picking on me? Would he call my mom and tell her I was a horrible student? Would he report me to Principal Schor? Would I be thrown back to the zoo?

Last period's bell sounded, and the class emptied. Noah jumped up, but Mr. Coursey asked him to wait a minute, too. We looked at each other again, and I wondered if we shouldn't set out for Mexico tonight.

"Misters Douglas and Baumgarten—"

"Mr. Coursey, I can't stay for detention today, I have He..."

"Hebrew class," Mr. Coursey's neck jiggled at Noah. "This is no detention. I want to speak to you both. I have a project as part of your penitence for the less than exemplary behavior you've shown all year. In addition to your term paper, I want you two to present a selection from the slavery novel 'Uncle Tom's Cabin,' by Harriet Beecher Stowe, whose family hails from this fair city."

"What?" Noah looked ill. "Mr. Coursey, I..."

"I know you're thrilled, since the two of you like to perform in class so much. The selection you choose must capture the essence of slavery, and I will be grading you on it, which means you will have to read the entire book, copies of which you'll find in the library. Mr. Douglas, do you understand?"

"Yes sir."

"Mr. Baumgarten?"

Noah nodded.

"A lesson well learned is one taken to heart. Truth to tell, I only recently overheard a teacher telling another teacher of this particular punishment. A novel idea, I think." His laugh consisted of several short grunts, like a wicked witch. "You only have five weeks before school lets out, so you best get busy. Mr. Baumgarten, you're excused."

Noah left. I thought I would piss my pants.

"Mr. Douglas. Do you live in Elmwood?"

"No, in Finlater."

"It's Find-laata."

I'd never in my life said anything curt or rude to an adult before, and "We say Finlater" slipped out of me of its own will. I was shocked that I said it.

"And we—and the citywide spelling bee—say Findlaata, as you found out so embarrassingly. With all due respect, your gibberish version is wrong, obviously."

Again, words marched forward as new tears boiled down my cheeks: "But sir, if they had pronounced the word the way I know it, I would have spelled it correctly. It's not fair."

"Dear child, life is terribly unfair. Now, you are a very bright young man, doubtless, and my best student, I'll grant you that, and it is because you have such promise that I give you the following advice: You must listen less at home and more at school, and find a less reprobate friend to consort with, since it is schooling that will earn you a ticket out of Find-laata."

"Thank you, sir."

I ran outside.

Noah was on the playground. "That fat bastard," Noah

shouted. I looked around to see if Mr. Coursey was behind us. No chance he would have heard us in the bedlam, kids zipping toward every exit. Our lockers were down at the other end of the hall.

"Last day of school, he's getting sugar in his gas tank."

"Yeah," I seconded.

Noah continued ranting. I saw Dudley leaning against the playground border fence with Santiago and a few other boys from our part of Finlater. They looked like troublemakers. I waved at him, but he didn't wave back.

"I gotta get Isaac and Leeza or my mom's going to kill me," Noah said. I'll call you tonight."

"Don't, I'll get in trouble." I said. "My mom doesn't let us talk on the phone. Maybe if I tell her it's about a school project, she might. Let me call you."

He took off across the playground.

I ran over to Dudley to tell him to wait for me. Dudley's fingers looped through the fence. The sole of his foot pushed into it too.

"I'm not going home yet," Dudley said. "You, Delrico and Corey go ahead."

"Okay, but tell 'em to wait, I'll be right back. I have to get a book at the library."

I didn't wonder what he was up to, with my own stuff too pressing. The library was on the second floor. I got the book, no problem. Mrs. Greenbacher, the septuagenarian librarian—her hair whipped up like mashed potatoes—said, "Don't know what Mr.

Coursey's thinking putting that kind of stuff in your head."

"Beats me." I had other urgent concerns. "Mrs. Greenbacher, what's a Jew?"

"Beg pardon?"

"What's a Jew? You know, Jewish?"

"It's a person who practices a religion that came from the Ancient Hebrews."

"What's that?"

"Semitic people."

"What's that?"

"Dessert people."

"What?"

"Well, they come from the Middle East."

"Huh?"

"Looky here, Mr. Douglas, the Jews were killed in the last world war, exterminated—that much you need to know if you know nothing else."

"The Holocaust."

"That's right. Now, you want to read up on that, help yourself, but we don't have books like that here. You'll have to go to the library downtown."

"Yes, ma'am, but can you tell me, can anybody join, be a Jew?"

"Well, I guess. I mean, it isn't like the Methodist or Lutheran faiths. But why would anybody want to join? With everybody hating them all."

"Why does everybody hate 'em?"

"Heaven only knows. I don't personally. Just like I never hated your people. As long as you weren't dirty and foul-mouthed."

Noah was right, Jews and blacks were the same.

"I don't hate 'em, I love 'em." I nearly shouted. "I would join. I will join."

"You and Sammy Davis, Jr., huh," she cackled.

"But I don't like him, my Grandpa Pleasant says he's an "Uncle Tom..."

"Well, to each his own," she said, waving me off with a veiny hand.

I didn't want to be like Sammy Davis, with his smashed nose and iguana smile. I ran to the playground, now emptied out in those few minutes I was in the library. Only Corey waited for me.

"Where's Delrico?"

"He left," Corey smirked. "Said he don't want to be around no honkie lover."

"A Jew lover," I said proudly. "Forget that cross-eyed fool."

Corey laughed. "You one messed up kid."

"Takes one to know one."

MOTHER HENS

Mr. Coursey's payback assignment drove me nuts. Cold terror, pure and simple, forced me headfirst into Stowe's book. I gave it my every free moment, and when I wasn't reading it I was thinking about reading it. Spelling, polynomial functions, and Asian capitals didn't matter. Mr. Coursey wasn't going to hold me back. I was going to the smart high school with Noah no matter what—the first step in becoming a Jew had to be sticking as close to my Jew, my SB, as possible. And if my brains failed me, and my plans didn't work out because Mr. Coursey flunked me, well, I was even prepared to play dirty. Putting sugar in his gas tank would be the first assault. Noah already had far worse dreamed up.

I was half-scared Mr. Coursey had called our moms. But Mom bought my version without question—that Mr. Coursey loved the theater and wanted to give us kids culture. I was given phone access to Noah with her blessings. I never mentioned anything about Noah's folks. I didn't bring up the house for sale either. Funny thing was, Noah stopped asking if I had asked, as if he knew. He was stalling, too. The only thing on his mind was his dad's store. He wouldn't say what was wrong, only that his father was in an "altered state." What did that mean—had Mr. Baumgarten turned into a liquid, a hamster, a monster, or gone crazy? "You really wanna help? Get your mom and your friends and everybody in your family to buy some clothes at Ben's." Ben's, Ben's, Ben's. It really was annoying. You'd have thought it was a matter of life and death. I didn't even know what to say. Our communication suddenly closed in on us. Torturing Mr. Coursey was our safest topic, other than Jimi Hendrix, Pink Floyd, the Jackson Five, and Mexico. There were things I kept to myself, and now I knew he had secrets, too.

With Dad at home during the day since he worked the third shift, every so often Mom volunteered for overtime. Thursday evening, Dad greeted us with the news that Mom was working extra. He usually never bothered to tell us what instructions she gave him for us. He had been on his way for a snack, and we just happened to be there. He was in his usual getup of tight bikini underwear that scrunched his privates into a tomato-like ball. The imitation silk tank top, red in this case, mashed his nipples. Moccasin slippers dragged when he crossed the room. A cigarette burned in his lips, his eyes twisted against the smoke. His hands balanced dirty dishes. He acted surprised to see us. If only he'd known, he'd have saved himself a trip.

"Damn." He released the dishes into the sink with a loud crash, and pried the cigarette from his lips. "Cliffy, you know anything about pork chops?"

What was there to know about rolling pork chops in boxed, seasoned breadcrumbs? It was pork chop Thursday, and lately Mom was using Shake 'n Bake, Dad's favorite. Stove Top Stuffing was also his favorite. I missed the Pork 'n Beans we used to eat. They went so well with regular old fried pork chops.

"Nothing at all. But I think there's directions on the box. I'd do it except I've got a lot of homework." Aside of being afraid of lighting the oven, I was determined to stick with Stowe even if we all wasted away to bones. Besides, Dad was the grown-up, and minding us was his job.

"Corey, Dudley—unless one of y'all know something about cooking, we won't be eating until late."

"I can't read," Corey said, laughing.

"Yeah, right." Dad grabbed a Colt 45 and green onion potato chips and an old chicken wing. He doused it with Red Devil hot sauce as if the bottle itself were burning hot. Cigarette ash dropped to the floor. "Corey, since you can't read, clean that up for your old man so you mama won't get on me," he said, his eyes squinty against the smoke. His slippers dragging the floor, he added, "All y'all do your homework like Cliffy there." Whether he was asking them if they had done their homework or telling them they should, it was hard to say.

Daddy's-boy Corey threw himself into soapsuds and dishwashing Dad's mess. Dudley muttered that he was going to Santiago's. I figured this was code for Maybelline's pootang. Corey pounced on the phone, refusing to get off so I could have my authorized call. Dad shouted downstairs for him to "get off and stay off the damn phone, boy."

Corey looked mad. Hushed curses swarmed the room like sweat bees. But Dad's place on Corey's pedestal was secure. Cartoons, especially Prince Planet, could still carry him away. Mom usually got home around nine after working overtime. She often brought Kentucky Fried Chicken on those nights. Feeling very hungry, I brought "Uncle Tom's Cabin" to the table with me, letting it sit in my lap. I felt close to starving and could barely concentrate when Mom finally rushed in at 9:30. She wobbled to the table cradling grocery sacks, but no Kentucky Fried Chicken. Her eyes blazed with an exhausted excitement. She had been dressing fashionably for work, too, since Dad's return. Her perky nurse-like factory uniform was hidden behind a yellow Pogue's coat with buttons like butter cookies.

"Sorry I'm late, there was a terrible accident on Vine."

"I was worried," I said. "Where's the chicken?"

"Worried about your stomach! There's White Castle's. There's another bag in Miss Glodine's car. Get it for me. And be sure to say thank you. Corey, tell your dad I'm home."

I ran outside, skipping the steps and instead speeding downhill toward the parking lot. Miss Glodine's Mercury Comet's fan belt made asthma-like wheezes. Miss Glodine and Mom had known each other since high school, although they weren't friends then, and according to Mom they weren't really friends now, although it was Miss Glodine who got Mom the job and was always available when Mom needed her. Near as I could tell, she just took pity on Mom, maybe because she herself had been dogged by a man. Her offers to carry us around to shop sometimes included a rant against men and the runts they stuck women with. Her prickly feelings were freely given to us kids too—since we'd probably grow into no-account dogs—especially when she had us alone, like when we had to fetch grocery bags. As I opened the door, Miss Glodine leaned sideways, like she was pulled down by the weight of her titties. She was as big as a Cincinnati Bengal linebacker and looked stuffed behind the wheel. She had recently given up her Diana Ross wig in favor of the shag. It gave her face a donut-like roundness but also a pincushion head. "Hi fella," she said, pushing the grocery bag at me. "It's just terrible how fast y'all growing up. I'm so glad I don't have no kids to kill me, even if they is cute."

I grabbed the grocery bag and ran. Inside, Mom was turning the gas stove on, bending down to light the pilot, that ring of fire I was terrified of.

"Thanks, Cliffy. There's some White Castle's warming in the oven. I'll go up and change." Loud enough so Corey could hear, Mom warned, "There better be twenty-five of them when I come back. Where's Dudley?"

"He went to Santiago's to get his geography book," I volunteered.

"A book, huh?"

Dudley walked in on cue, just as Mom rounded the stairwell. I figured he was hanging out nearby and had seen Miss Glodine's car pull up. "I was just about to call over to Santiago's for you."

"Hey Mom," he gruffed.

"I don't see a geography book."

"Huh?"

"Go set the table. You're on dishes tonight. You're getting off easy. We're having White Castle's."

As soon as her feet clunked on the stairs, the onion rings and

French fries began to dwindle, straight from the oven's mouth into Corey's.

"Cliffy, what you tell her?" Dudley bounded over to me in a huff.

"Just what you told me, that you were going to Santiago's. I added the geography book for authenticity."

He went for an onion ring. "Next time, pick a subject I'm good at."

"Like what?" I asked.

"Like… like…"

"Pootang?"

I thought he was still mad at me from a few Sundays ago, so his laughter surprised me. The smallness and meanness of his teenage self broke away like bug chrysalis. He made like he was going to strangle me, only this time it was in fun. We staggered around the kitchen together, liking each other once again. It was brief, though. Dad's feet pounding the stairs restored him to misery. Hate-filled eyes watched as Dad took over the kitchen for his share of White Castle's. Dad accused Mom of trying to "starve us to death. And Lacey, stop putting so much starch on my shirt; the collar like to cut me." Then off he went, slippers dragging the floor. Dudley shook his head.

We sat down to White Castle's and Mom's questions about our day. I still had the Stowe book in my lap, and was about to tell Mom about it when the phone rang. She went to the living room to take the call.

"Cliffy, will you come in here."

I did. She pressed the receiver into her chest.

"There's a Laura Baum-something on the phone, your friend Noah's mother?"

"It's Baumgarten, and yes, ma'am."

"Is there something you want to tell me?"

"Well… Mrs. Baumgarten said she wanted to meet you and I thought…"

Mom glared at me. I was about to run, but she told me to wait.

"Sorry," Mom said into the receiver. "You were saying about the assignment?" Her face scrunched up. "Cliffy didn't say anything about him and Noah acting up in class. He just said the teacher was into acting and theater stuff."

She shook her head as she said "I agree. If they weren't disrespecting the teacher they wouldn't have to do the extra work."

When her mouth sagged, I knew punishment was coming.

"Cliffy knows better than that… No, Cliffy doesn't have anything but chores this weekend, and extra ones for acting up in class… Spend the night?… I don't know. I'll have to ask my husband… Okay… Nice talking to you too… Likewise… A what?… A house… No, Cliffy didn't say anything about a house… Well, sure, we'd like to see it… I'll speak to my husband about… Huh-huh… You're very welcome… Goodnight."

"Cliffy, what white friends you got that their mother calls over here to tell me about some trouble you in at school?"

"Mom..."

"What house you looking at in Elmwood that she's got to tell me about?"

"Mom..."

"When were you looking at a house?"

"Mom..."

"Cliffy, you better have some good answers."

"I'm trying to tell you, but you keep cutting me off." I could hear Dudley snickering from the kitchen sink.

"I'm waiting..."

"Okay," I said. My heart beat in my throat. "I told you before about my friend Noah, and you just forgot. He lives in Elmwood. When Dad first came back, I told Noah about it, because I was so proud"—I could see Mom pleased at the mention of Dad—"and I told Noah that we were going to move into our own house. That's what you said, Mom, when Dad came back, we were going to get our own house and I could have my own room. Remember?"

"I remember."

"Then Noah said he knew of a nice house that would be perfect for us, with enough bedrooms so me, Corey, and Dudley could have our own rooms, and we would have a yard, and could have a dog, and we wouldn't have to go to different schools and me and Noah could be best friends forever..."

"Okay," she said.

"Mom, I thought you wanted a house, and I wanted to help us find one."

Just then Dad yelled downstairs for Mom to bring his uniform.

"Corey, go upstairs and tell you father that I'll bring his suit with me when I come up."

Maybe because she seemed so tired, Mom lost her thoughts.

"That was real sweet, Cliffy, but…"

"I'm sorry for disrespecting Mr. Coursey, but we were talking about the house, when you and Dad could come and look at it."

"I see," she said. "It was wrong and disrespectful. Did you apologize?"

"No, ma'am."

"I want you to apologize first thing tomorrow."

"I will, Mom."

"You and…"

"Noah…"

"…Noah and you will have to work on that book project together, and Mrs. Baumgarden says you can stay at their place this weekend so you and Noah can practice."

At this, she shook her head, grinning, as if the idea of her son staying with white people in Elmwood seemed to defy good sense. "You really want to spend the night with them?"

"Yes, ma'am."

"I don't even know those people," she said.

"Mom, Mrs. Baumgarten is very nice. They're Jewish people."

"Jewish?"

"Yeah. From the Ancient Hebrews, you know, Semitic

people."

"It's the Jews that killed Christ, but they've been very nice to our people..."

"What?" Mom didn't know arithmetic well, so I figured she didn't know history, either.

"It's true."

"Maybe it was an accident. Like Delrico killing his sister."

She seemed to consider it. "Years ago, before you were born, your daddy's mother used to cook for very rich ones and they were good to her, give her a car and everything. And you know those boys, Werner, Chaney, and Goodman, two of them, I forget which, were Jewish and they died trying to get us civil rights. Guess they can't be all bad."

"The Baumgartens are the best." Then I added. "Mr. Baumgarten was a Freedom Rider too, and everything and he's been all over the world. He owns Ben's downtown and he said he would give Dad a nice discount. Dad's heard of it, too, Mom. He told me."

"That's a nice store," she said. Then she said, more to herself, "Baumgarden, why do I think I know that name?"

That's Baumgarten, I said to myself, wondering if I should correct her pronunciation. Instead I said "And Father's Day's coming up soon."

"What a thoughtful gentleman I've raised," she said, kissing my forehead. She always said that when I did something that really pleased her.

Pushing it for what it was worth, I added, "I want to make you and Mr. Coursey proud, and we'll do the best 'theatrics.'"

"Mrs. Baumgarden seems like a good person. I'll ask your father." She turned to go upstairs. I told her to wait a minute. I ran over to the water heater area, where she hung their work uniforms to dry at night. I grabbed one, then intercepted her halfway upstairs.

"You forgot this, Mom."

"Oh, thank you, Cliffy. Your mom's just pooped out now."

She continued upstairs, then said. "Okay. You can go. I don't need your dad's permission. I know you'll represent us well."

"I will, Mom, I promise."

Once she was out of sight, I did a victory lap around the living room and back to the kitchen.

"Big head." Dudley banged plates together as he dried them.

"Pussy breath," I smirked.

We giggled.

"You got me good again," he said. "I know you been running up to see that white boy, so I'm telling you, don't go to the park Saturday."

"Why?"

"You might get hurt. Just stay away."

My crazy brother. I went upstairs with my book. The park was not my worry.

How was I going to tell Noah about Bikini Dad?

mAn ChilD

The morning was sunny-side-up bright. I left early to intercept Noah again, only this time he was waiting a block from his house. I wanted a muffin and juice, just like last time, and to thank his mother for calling mine.

"Dang, you sure are slow."

"Whatcha waiting out here for?"

"For you, knucklehead."

I couldn't tell if he was mad or what. I grinned when I noticed the bicycle. Not the one with the banana seat. This one had a baseball glove seat, big enough only for one person. We assumed our positions and I stared at a sliver of skin like vanilla ice cream above his underwear. I wanted to hold on to him there, but as we fumbled into motion my hands clutched our book bags and we tilted further off balance. The car we sideswiped kept us from hitting ground.

He jerked the bike upright. "You pedal, and I'll carry our bags."

We tried it again, with the same results, only we capsized, hitting the street in a thud.

"Let's go back for the other bike."

"No, it's got a flat," he barked, shoving me aside, then pushing himself up. "Fuck it, let's just walk."

"Something the matter?"

I looked up in time to see Noah's mom. The familiar station wagon snailed along through the school zone. Sunlight showered down through the tree shade like rain. I could see Mrs. Baumgarten wasn't her usual plain self. Her hair was done up in a flip and she was wearing pancake and lipstick. A figure slumped in the passenger seat, just outside the wedge of sunshine lighting Mrs. Baumgarten. It was Noah's father in the front seat, his head against the neck rest as if he were asleep. Leeza and Isaac were in the backseat, as still as mannequins.

I put my hand up to wave, but Noah jerked it down.

"Don't," he ordered.

I nearly said, Get off me. "SB, what's the matter?"

"My dad's really sick this morning." Noah looped our book bags by their straps over the handlebar.

"What's the matter with him?"

He stared at me, his lips smushed together showing the notches of the braces.

"It's none of your business."

"I thought we were best friends."

"We are." He kicked the bike. "But you lied to me about your dad. My mom talked to your mom last night. Why'd you lie?"

"I'm sorry. I didn't mean to. I didn't have a dad before March second. Before that, he didn't exist. Well, he did exist, only I didn't know him. I swear. I made up my Los Alamos dad because I felt bad. I figured I should have a dad, a good dad. Then my real dad showed up..."

"Is he that bad?"

"He wears zebra-striped bikini underwear."

"Pukey." Noah said, his lips almost smiling.

"All he cares about is his Thunderbird. I don't think he even likes us. I want a dad like yours, not like him."

Noah turned full on me. "No, you don't. He's…" The tears jumped from his eyes.

"SB, what's the matter?"

"My dad's sick. Heart sick. Mom's taking him to the hospital now."

"Is it Ben's? I'm sorry we didn't go buy anything. We can't."

"It's okay," he sniffled. "He gets like that sometimes. He'll get better. He always does in a few days. He's the best dad, except when he's sad."

"I still want a dad just like yours."

Noah grinned and I could see sprinkles of blood on his lips.

"Any other lies, soul brother?"

"No, that's it."

"I got a punishment for you for lying."

"What's that?"

"You'll see." He laughed like Boris Karloff.

"I'm scared. Don't hurt me."

He seemed happy-go-lucky again. "I can't wait till you come over. We can milk it all night, until our dicks fall off."

"I bet I got more than you."

We wagered a Snickers bar, sealing the deal by linking our left pinkies.

"Maybe my dad'll be okay by then."

"I hope so."

Lying wasn't a good thing, I realized. In Mr. Coursey's class I was about to scribble a note to Noah swearing off lying forever.

The hated teacher was deep in Gettysburg, reading the endless address. His voice rising and falling, trembling with emotion. It seemed he was about to cry.

"Misters Douglas and Baumgarten," he said.

I looked up from my book, startled.

"I just want to say we look forward to the dramatic presentation you will favor us with."

"Yes, sir," I said.

"Now," Mr. Coursey scanned the room, "I should say, before we get back to the subject at hand, that I haven't forgotten you other menaces, Jenny Weisburger, Nathan Brucker, Kenneth Pringle…"

At the end of class, the other "menaces" were given poetry assignments. They had to research poets writing during the Civil War, and had to do a presentation for or against the institution of slavery. Good! We'd all be humiliated and flunked together, as I saw it, then the school would fire Mr. Coursey for meanness to students.

"The grievous offenders, misters Douglas and Baumgarten, would appear to have the easier task, since they will not have to spend all their time in the library, or begging their parents for help, as you no doubt will, but I assure you, theirs is the harder task. Correct, Mr. Douglas?"

"Yes sir."

Noah nodded.

Outside, Noah said, "Oh how I hate that fat fucker."

"Fat swine fucker."

Noah started walking in the opposite direction of home.

"Where you going?"

"My secret place. Follow me."

"What about Leeza and Isaac?"

"What about 'em? And what about your brothers?"

"Fuck 'em," I said. I'd just tell Mom we got held up after class.

We crossed Winton Road, with its highway-like traffic and mysterious turns into and away from the city. Sure, I'd seen the street before, but turned back in fear of what lay beyond it—a big empty nothing. Not now—I was up for anything. For the first time, I noticed a large house sitting on a small hill just beyond the wide road. We climbed the hill, and it seemed like there was little beyond it, just rolling hills yellowed with daffodils, a curling road and trees far off in the distance. It was a pretty place, postcard-perfect. Noah pointed to an area past a barn, and we ran through grass and low brush, until we neared a wedge in the ground where a small stream flowed into a pond.

After sneezing, Noah said "Nobody ever comes over here. This is my own special spot. I catch tadpoles, and I smoke cigarettes, or do anything else I want." He pulled a cigarette from his pocket and plopped down on the ground.

"Where you get that?"

"I have my own pack." He held up Larks.

"Wow," I was impressed. A whole pack. Me and Delrico tried smoking and I didn't like it all. When Noah lit one, he handed it to me for a puff. I took it, sucked on it, coughed and gave it back.

"You know what I wanna learn?"

"What?"

"Flying," he said. "If I could fly, we'd be in Mexico right now."

"We could go anywhere."

"Where would you want to go?"

"Maybe Alaska, that's where Big Foot is."

"Yeah, that would be cool."

"I'd like to see New York."

"Real cool," Noah shouted. "I used to live in New York."

"You lying."

"I swear on my Atom Ant collection. I was born there and we lived there until I was five. My dad moved us here. He inherited the store from my Uncle Ben Irving, who my father was named after. My full name is Ben Noah Irving Baumgarten the third. My dad used to stay with him in the summer and he worked in the shop. My Uncle Ben was murdered in Israel."

"Why?"

"Because those people are dogs," he carped and then spat. "Anyway, Uncle Ben left the place to my dad. After my dad came home from Nam, we came here. It was just me then. I love New

York. I never wanted to live here. It's so boring. I can't wait for the holidays because that's when we get to go back."

"Must be fun."

"You'd like New York. That's where we should go. First Mexico, then New York."

"Okay."

As he told me about the subways, pizza and stickball, he pulled his shoes off. He put his foot in my lap.

I protested, "Ugh, I don't want your toe jam."

"I'm a freak. Scary, huh?"

The baby toe and the one next to it were webbed together.

"I'm part amphibian." He ran into the pond. "Come on in."

The water was clear, but I hesitated.

"Come on," he said.

I pulled off my shoes and reluctantly followed him. The water went just above our ankles, and was ice-box cold. We walked down to the mouth of the pond, the water rising to our calves. He kneeled to look for tadpoles, or so he said, and the next I knew he'd grabbed my legs and lifted me up like he was going to throw me in the water.

"Don't, my mom'll kill me," I shouted.

Okay, he said, but he staggered suddenly and lost balance. We teetered and then fell with a splash. Turning in the cold water to stand up, I shouted "shit" and he laughed and coughed. What else could I do but laugh and curse. "You did that on purpose."

"Soul brother, I tripped. Honestly."

"I'm gonna get killed, you never gonna see me again."

"I really am sorry."

But he wasn't sorry, and we laughed harder.

"You're nuts," I said.

"That was one of your punishments for lying about your dad."

"One. What's the other?"

He pulled his now-white and shriveled dick out.

"You have to put your mouth on it before I milk it."

"Are you crazy, I'm not doing that."

"Pull yours out."

I did. It was cold and wet but that didn't stop it from getting hard.

He bent down and put his mouth on me. A sensation I'd never felt before took my breath. My knees nearly buckled by the time he stopped.

"See, it feels good, huh?"

"Yeah," I moaned.

"Do me. But don't bite."

His reddened and thickened so much I couldn't get my mouth around it, but he seemed to like it. He pulled his pants all the way down, and pushed his thing deeper into my mouth until I gagged.

"Stop it," I said.

"Sorry, it just feels so good. Lick it like a sucker."

It didn't taste like a sucker, but I liked licking it and hearing his "yeah, yeah." It was like a frankfurter cooked so long the top splits open. I licked the split and that's when I tasted his gism. It was sweeter than before. I stood up. We looked at each other, grinning, and for the first time I worried that I was going to hell. This definitely wasn't something I should be doing. But I'd have to worry about my soul later. For now, all bets were on Noah my soul brother.

We milked it, each shooting his gism into the pond.

"God that feels so good, don't it."

"God!" I searched the sky for lightning, knowing we would be struck. I pulled my pants up. "Do Jews believe in hell?"

"Hell, yeah."

HOT WATER

I could never even imagine what a cocksucker did, but now I knew that I was one. If found out, I was dead meat. Mom would kill me. My brothers, too. Everybody I knew would beat me in the streets, with all the available skillets, belts and curses they could find.

The Thunderbird wasn't in the parking lot. Nobody seemed around, but I flew through the house, straight to the bathroom mirror, convinced my mouth bore some new mark. Visualizing the act that would cast me into eternal damnation, I started to sweat, and the ice-cold bath water hardly bothered me as I plunged in, sticking my head under the suds. I could nearly feel Noah's mouth on me. Next I knew, I had a hard-on, again.

Mom wasn't home, either. I realized this only when I came downstairs. Neither were Corey and Dudley. I was alone. I threw my clothes into the washing machine, adding other clothes so Mom wouldn't get suspicious. Then I called Noah.

His mom answered. "Hi Cliffy. I really like your mom."

"She likes you, too."

"I got it, Mom," Noah said. "Hey, soul brother. Hold on." I heard a few clicks on the line. "You alright? You ran like a bat out of hell."

"I told you I was gonna get killed."

"I'm talking to a corpse then?"

"Not yet. Any news on your dad?"

"A little better," he said. "He's back on his drugs."

"I'm glad."

"Boy, that was fun this afternoon."

I didn't say anything.

"Soul brother, you're the coolest friend I ever had. I can't wait till we hang out with each other all the time."

"Me too."

I heard the back door slam. It was just stupid Corey. I told Noah I'd see him in the morning.

"Hey Cliffy, you believe we're all alone," Corey grinned. Seeing the phone free, he got on and then ran outside. I went upstairs with Stowe, and tried to concentrate. But all I could think about was the afternoon. It seemed like I got a hard-on every ten minutes over the next few hours. By bedtime my dick was burning from friction, and milked bone dry, and still I wanted to do it.

Mom finally came home around nine. She'd apparently told Dad about working overtime, and he'd forgotten. She was furious that I was the only one of her kids home. It didn't matter that Corey and Dudley came inside within minutes of her arrival. Muttering and cursing to herself, she banged pots and pans around. I went upstairs to read. By the time Dad rolled in, at ten-thirty, she'd blown a gasket.

From us kids' room, I heard Mom shout. "Cliff, I can't believe you forgot and left the boys home to run wild. I come home at nine and Dudley and Corey are not even here. You said you would be here. I would never have done the overtime if you hadn't said you'd be here."

"What's the big deal? You act like they're five-year-olds. Stop treating them like a bunch of girls."

"And whatcha doing? Nothing. And what have you done? Nothing. For ten years you didn't do so much a send a nickel to raise your boys, so don't tell me how to raise 'em now. You have no right to say shit. All I asked was for you to be here. That's it."

"Lacey…"

"…just to do something that I shouldn't even have to ask you to do, something your ass should do just because you're their father."

"Lacey…"

"You're in hot water with me."

There was a funny silence—funny because I thought he'd grab and kiss her, and that would be the end of it. Only it wasn't.

Then came: "I know this, Lacey, you best get out of my damn face."

He must have pushed her because she shouted "Don't touch me."

Then I heard Mom say "Dudley, sit down. This doesn't concern you."

Dad said "Dudley, you better get outta my face before I break it." Then came a slapping sound.

"Don't you hit him," Mom screamed.

My heart sped up so fast I thought it would burn rubber out of my chest. I was about to run to the stairs, until I heard Dad's feet pounding them. Was he going to hurt her? Hurt us? I was scared.

He went into their room, crashed and banged around. A few minutes later he emerged and pounded the stairs again. I heard nothing more after the back door slam, until much later when Mom was crying in their room.

Dudley came to bed with a slap-swollen face, swearing he would "kill that Nigga."

Corey said, "You shouldna opened your big mouth."

"And let him push my Mom! Naw, hell naw!"

"You gonna get hurt. It's their business," Corey added, but his voice was shaky, close to crying.

I didn't say a word. What was there to say? It seemed to me, I wouldn't be in hell alone—our whole household was already booked there, too.

Mom took Dudley into her room for a talk. I went downstairs for a knife. I put it under my pillow and tried to sleep. I could hear Dudley cussing all night in his dreams. "See, I toldya, that motherfucker... He ain't shit. Ain't shit."

HARD LUCK

I ran to Noah's with a sore, swollen dick. I was ready to detour to the pond to suck his wiener and have him suck mine, and then for us two to sprint to New York or Mexico, leaving my fucked-up family behind. But Noah came to the back porch before I reached the door. I guess he'd been waiting for me.

"Let's go now."

"Everything okay?"

"No, it ain't." His eyes were swollen and he looked deprived of sleep.

"What's the matter?"

He didn't answer until we were a block away from his house.

"Noah, please, what's the matter?"

"Well… My Dad ran off in the middle of the night—in his shitty underpants from him crapping on himself, can you believe it! The police found him all covered in dirt and do-do, and they took him in. He's going back to the hospital again."

"Why he run off?"

"He doesn't know what he's doing. He's really messed up this time. He's been in the hospital before, but I don't know… I'm scared, Cliffy, I'm really scared."

Then Noah cried. His face puckered and turned bright red. He made dog-like whining sounds. I put my arm around him, and then I began to cry and get a hard-on at the same time.

A car drove by and someone shouted: "Look at the Jew-Nigger lovebirds."

Noah broke free of me, and went for a rock to throw.

"Fucking bastards," he screamed.

We were dry-eyed when we reached the school courtyard.

"So, me bawling like a baby gives you a hard-on, huh?"

"You wanna skip school?"

"No… I mean I want to… but I promised my mom. She's supposed to call if there's any news."

I was in homeroom when his name came over the loudspeaker. I imagined Noah scared and worried, heading toward the principal's office as if he were boarding the Hindenburg. Was it about his dad? I prayed to the God I didn't give a hoot about, and hoped for the best. I didn't see Noah again that afternoon. He didn't call me that night. I called but got their recorded voices (mostly Leeza's) singing out that I should leave a message on their new answering machine—I'd never even heard there was such a machine! I hung up, full of awe, but soon I worried myself into sleeplessness. I wanted to rush to his place first thing in the morning, but I fell asleep at the last minute and completely overslept, with barely enough time to make it to homeroom.

Noah didn't show up at school that morning. At lunchtime I broke a school rule. I slipped outside our little campus and ran to Noah's place. No one was home. Cupcake lay on the porch like a throw rug. She stirred when she saw me, shifting onto front paws as if about to tap dance, came over for a sniff and pet, then retired again. A note on the front door requested that Herb the milkman delay orders until further notice and that Noble the mailman pile mail into the basket until the weekend, when they would hopefully return from a family situation in New York. Who was taking care of Cupcake, I wondered—and where was the note for me!

I thought I would go crazy. My head ached with missing Noah. Heartsickness stole my concentration throughout the day, along with my appetite. My dick hurt bad from all the attention I now paid it. I must have looked a 13-year-old wreck, stumbling around like the drunks we saw from the bus on our way for groceries in Avondale.

Next day, Mr. Coursey eyed me with what felt like pure meanness. He made it clear he expected one or both of us to deliver our dramatics, no matter what. "Mind you, giving a monologue is the true test of the actor—I'm sure you will not disappoint us."

"No sir," I said, wanting to point out that I'm not an actor, just a Jew-loving, spelling-bee-hating, yellow black boy from a neighborhood with a name white people pronounce one way and black people another. Everything was messed up. Noah and I had done nothing about the Elmwood house or the school test I had to take to get to the new smart school. What was I supposed to do—a helpless, dumb kid dependant on everybody for everything?

Thursday night, a phone call from kind Mrs. Baumgarten somewhat put me out of my misery. She and Mom spoke. The phone was not handed to me, much to my deepening misery.

"Mrs. Baumgarden said you can't come this weekend. They've had to go to New York. Her husband's father had a heart attack and died real sudden. You can visit next weekend."

"Okay." I wondered if Noah was sitting beside his Mom—anxious to speak to me, too.

"She said her husband isn't taking it well. Poor man."

I figured Mr. Baumgarten would really go crazy now, and so would Noah.

"She sounds like a very nice lady. She told me to call her Lor. I told her she can call me Lacey."

"I've been telling you she's really nice. Did you know she's a lawyer?"

"No," Mom said.

"She's from New York City."

"Smart women in New York City. We got a cousin up there, you know. She graduated from Columbia University—this would be Grandpa's niece Lindsey. I haven't seen her in years."

"Maybe you can be a lawyer like her."

"Right. Wouldn't that be something?"

"Someday I'll be rich and I'll take care you, Mom. You won't have to depend on anybody. Nobody'll ever hurt you."

"Of all you kids, I bet you will." She cupped my face with her hand. I wanted her to hug me, I wanted to be a little boy in her arms again. "I raised you just fine, I think."

Then she added, "White people ain't all bad, but there's something that don't mix about black and white. I don't know what it is."

Dad came home with fresh flowers and an apology. He

announced he was tired of homemade fried chicken. He brought home Swanson's frozen kind, which alone was reason to have a grudge against him forever, I figured. He then went upstairs for a talk with Dudley. Mom shoved the frozen tray into the oven, her nose upturned.

Before following him, she said, "We're just different from them."

"But Mom, math is different from art, but I like both."

"Not me. I didn't like either one. To each his own, I guess."

That was also true of chicken, we soon found out.

wHIte PeE

Delrico and me patched things up. It happened a couple mornings after Noah left town. Our little gang to school gathered down on the flat part of King's Run Drive—Santiago, Dudley, Corey, and a couple other kids. I could see on Dudley and Santiago's faces that they had better things to do, like screwing Maybelline. They stared in the direction of her house, opposite that of school.

Me and Delrico fell into step with a shy "hey."

I was the more mature of us. "What's going on?"

"SOS, you tell me."

"Well, I got this stupid assignment to do for history class, and I have to read this book about slavery called 'Uncle Tom's Cabin.'"

"I heard of that."

The liar. "And then I have do a 'theatrics.'"

"What's that?"

"It's when you make like you an actor, you know, like Paul Newman."

"Who he?"

"You know, Butch Cassidy and the Sundance Kid."

"Oh," he said.

"That awful teacher Mr. Coursey is going to make me do the 'theatrics' by myself if Noah doesn't come back soon. Boy, I hate him."

"I've been reading, too."

"What book?"

We let ourselves lag further behind the gang. Delrico pulled from his back pocket a few folded pages from his reading assignment. Pictures of a naked white lady's titties and pussy! Lynching material, definitely!

I'd seen contraband coochies on Playboy Bunnies before, each of the ladies with plumes of platinum blond hair and Marilyn Monroe beauty moles. This wasn't that kind of pretty woman on a pretty bed in a pretty bedroom. No, her face was hard and weather-beaten, and her titties sagged in the direction of due South. Her stomach was rubbery and her legs spread like a stepladder. The room looked like an auto repair shop. Her pussy like a slice of burned crumb pie. The next page showed a hairy man standing in a doorway, with his reddish dick poking out of the fly of his blue underwear. It seemed like he was staring right at me with a big grin on his face that made me blush and tingle with goose bumps. The next page showed her cock-sucking. His open mouth making a strange face—and probably slobbering. I could almost feel Noah's mouth on me. I wondered if I looked like her when I cock-sucked. Did Noah look like her? The last page showed the man atop her, sticking it in, his butt the color of raw chicken.

"That's real pootang and fucking," Delrico said, big-eyed. "Man, I be making white pee every time I look at that pussy."

"Yeah." I was truly awed. "Where you get them from?"

"Santiago got 'em. Notice the writing. It's Swedish."

"Wow." Now my estimation of stupid Santiago went up, to

have got hold of such pictures.

"And the rest of the book?"

"No, this is it."

He wouldn't let me keep them. But throughout the school day the picture of the grinning man stayed in my mind. I wondered what it would be like to suck his wiener. It looked really big and smelly and choking. I kept picturing him getting out of a tub, and waiting in a door entry for me and Noah. I wasn't afraid. Noah said "No way José! Mine is the only one you put in your mouth."

Later, on my way home from school, I ran to Noah's house, just to see it and be close to him. I kept thinking that something must be wrong with me. I was hot, but had no fever.

Saturday, Delrico dropped by. At first I wanted to stay home in case Noah called, but Delrico had more Swedes. We went down to the creek in the woods beyond his house. We were overcome by a gang of pussies and titties, as we sat on a branch in our favorite tree. But there weren't any more pictures like the grinning man. Delrico didn't mind one bit.

"Boy, jerking off feels good, don't it." Delrico dug in his pants.

"Sure does."

"You be jerking off with that Jew?"

"What's it to you?"

"Nothing. Now he out of town, you got time for your Niggers."

"You talking crazy."

"Want to?"

"Want to what?"

"Jerk off?"

"I can't. My dingaling's cut."

"So! Mine's too. Mine's all cut up, and burns like hell. Come on."

"Naw, it hurts too much."

The branch Delrico straddled curled upward. He pulled his out, and it looked retarded, with a wrinkly skin over the head like sausage casing. Bikini Dad's was like that too, only way bigger. Delrico's grew as big as the grinning man's. I wondered if I should suck it. But he would be after me all the time. I laughed to myself, but pulled mine out anyway, and we jerked until we were hollering out loud.

Afterward, he leaned back, his legs dangling like sticks. Owls hooted and a magpie circled overhead, peering down at the rust-colored creek. Further upstream, catfish crawled along the muddy creek bottom. In the past we hooked a few with our homemade fishing poles. Mom refused to cook anything caught in that creek, and forbid us to swim in it, too. Downstream the surface bubbled and frothed, as if full of soap powder. The P&G plant had something to do with this, according to the news.

"Where's that Jew boy anyway?"

"Noah's at his grandfather's funeral in New York."

"New York? He from there, too?"

"Yep."

"I wanna go back to New York."

"You remember anything?"

"Naw, but Santiago do. He remembers the subway trains. He said it was fun riding underground, and the subway trains screech real loud like dinosaurs. He say his buddies used to climb on top, and ride through the tunnels with nothing to hold on. Kids got killed, he say."

"I wanna go to New York someday, too—but not to do that."

"You still my best friend," he said.

"Cool," I said, then added "until hell freezes over." We shook hands, adding a prolonged pinky lock. I didn't say he was my best friend. He was a best friend. It was something that both my best friends were from New York.

Delrico read comic books while I read Stowe. I was almost finished. The book made me think. I thought about the times we froze waiting on the bus. The time Mom lost her job and we ate eggs and toast for dinner. The nasty powdered milk we got from Salvation Army. We were hungry until Grandpa found out about Mom's job and gave her enough money until we got welfare. We suffered, but it was nothing like what Topsy, Harry, or Uncle Tom suffered. Poor Uncle Tom—I fast realized that being Bikini Dad's servant was nothing compared to broken-down Uncle Tom's situation. It must be just awful to be surrounded by people who only pretend to care about you when they don't really care at all.

White people sure seemed evil, even the good Christian ones. Maybe what Mom was saying about whites and blacks not mixing was true in a way. Maybe white and black people just don't really care about each other, when push comes to shove. Maybe white people only pretend to care about black people, but don't really, and black people can't do much but hate them for it. This school putting all us black kids into the zoo, whether we were smart or not. That is until Principal Schor, like the Abolitionists who were ready to die because they cared so much about freeing the slaves, came along. Seems like everybody in the world pretends to care about something they don't really care about. Bikini Dad—did he really care about us or was he just pretending? Mom—she couldn't have loved Mr. Porter since she dropped him like a hot potato the second Dad came along. Me—what was I pretending to care about? I wondered, as I penciled passages that might work for our dramatics. Noah was all I cared about, so I guess everything else was pretending.

And Delrico—what about him?

"Hey Dell, do you pretend like you care about something but you really don't?"

"What you mean?"

"Like peas—you eat them and make like they good so you don't get yelled at."

"Shit, I guess I pretend about everything then."

"Don't you really care about nuttin?"

"Pootang."

"Come on."

"Music. I like music. I just wish I could get my own sax. Thinking about taking one from school."

"I hope you don't get busted."

"Well." He sighed. "What about you?"

"I don't care about my brothers," I said, half-joking. "What about your sister? Did you care about her?"

"I don't know. I don't really remember. She was pretty like my mom. Very hairy and she had a nose like a button. I still see her."

"I bet she loved you."

"I don't know." He sighed again. "What else you pretend to care about?"

"I used to love school, but now I don't know…"

"You gotta get over the spelling bee, Cliffy."

"It ain't that."

"You been a nutjob ever since that damn bee. They tricked you. Niggers talk one way, Honkies another. Shit, if I was as smart as you, I'd really care about school. How else you gonna get outta Finlater?"

He was right, I realized. Right then and there I was over the spelling bee. It was history.

We lazed the afternoon away, just like we did so many summers past. He spotted mud turtles crawling around the creek shore. Some kids we knew crushed them with rocks. Delrico and I would never do that. That's what I liked about Delrico, he wasn't hurtful, even if he had killed his sister, and even if he could be spiteful. Maybe that's why he wasn't hurtful—he took his meanness out in spitefulness. I remember he said, "Turtles got a right to be left alone."

Bullies trawled the creeks, too. We were always on the lookout. I considered telling him about the knife I now slept with. But he might use it against me in the future.

At home, Mom was taking apart the kitchen looking for the butcher knife, her hair bound up in a daisy-printed kerchief. I pretended not to know what she was talking about, and that I had something pressing to attend to. I stayed in my room with the door locked. I pulled the knife out from under the mattress and placed it under my pillow, its home while I slept, and whenever Dad was around. The blade both comforted and terrified me—I felt safer with it there, yet I would sleep as still as a corpse, afraid of being stabbed in a sudden move. But I slept with it anyway, because I felt I was among enemies, people capable of turning on you, and certainly choking and beating on you. Mostly I kept it for Dudley, to use to stab Bikini Dad, in case he tried to hurt us. Only I didn't tell Dudley about it. I pictured myself handing him the weapon in a life or death moment, when, say, Dad had him by the throat and was choking him to within seconds of his life. Then murder would be justified, that's the way I saw it. But I guess I also kept it in case Dudley tried to hurt me and I had to defend myself. Although it was easier for me to see Dudley drawing my blood than me his.

At church I was scared. I thought that God on the cross was

going to cast me down as a cocksucker. That if He didn't hurl a thunderbolt to take me out, the choir would sing a chorus branding me a homo-sinner and humiliate me forever, a punishment far worse than my embarrassment and wounded pride over my spelling bee loss, which somehow, now, seemed silly to me. Over the loud voices of my paranoia, I heard Father Ferdinand's sermon about the sin of Godlessness. The Fall of the Grecian empire was due to the wicked ways of man, his weakness for vice and sexual perversion—coveting his brother's wife, "man laying down with man… Our brethren the Jews knew, for they had read the Book of David." What did that mean? Maybe the Jews were nicer to cocksuckers like me? Still, each time Father's voice stirred doom, my time felt up. I shrank in the pew, ready for misery's end. I had wanted to speak with him about the Jews. I had been willing to endure his pinches even, but not now.

After church, Father Ferdinand sought Mom out. I guess our spotty attendance required an explanation, or Mom's bold red lipstick had summoned him over for a chat. He was yam-colored, and his lips were calico-pink where color had faded away. He bowed his head as he approached us, his Afro like cotton balls. His "Hello, Cliffy" was enough to send me flying out the door.

Mom witnessed my hell-worthy rudeness and delivered her own thunderbolt: "Clifford Romel Douglas, go in there an apologize to Father Ferdinand right now."

I did, while he was in the middle of a conversation with blue-haired old ladies in chocolate mink. "I'm sorry," I shouted, and ran back outside.

Surprise of surprises, the Thunderbird was purring at the curb in front of the church, Dad poised for a Kodak moment. Mom probably mentioned we were going to Grandpa and Grandma Douglas', not to Grandpa and Grandma Pleasant's, who, I forgot, were in Memphis that weekend. Us kids never liked going to our other grandparents, but we had no choice. Mom didn't like going either, and didn't seem happy even now, as she criticized me again for being rude to Father Ferdinand, while we all piled into the car. The only person happy to be going was Dad. He turned the Isley Brothers eight track up, drowning us out and gathering a few damnable stares from the newly blessed.

Grandpa and Grandma Pleasant didn't like Dad, but Grandpa and Grandma Douglas sure loved Mom. Especially Grandma Douglas—her near-constant grieving over Mom and Dad not being together topped the reasons we hated going over there. She had the ruthless focus of a bedbug, burrowing its way into your will and breaking it. Reconciliation was what Grandma had wanted all along, as she told us over and over again, and as far as I know Dad's return might have been owing to her. Just before Dad turned up we had seen the Douglases more often than usual. Grandma Douglas had to have a titty removed. Mom said she had breast cancer, and she was lucky to be alive, and still might yet die. Die of complaining, Mom said.

She was a big woman, as wide and as tall as a twin bed, with, before cancer, titties like large pillows. Her hair was the blue of

Tidy Bowl toilet water, and her face was freckled with moles like birdseed. She was bossy and hateful (Mom would say) with a forked tongue. Everything was just fine, yet nothing was ever right. After greeting us with a wet Lipton-iced-tea kiss her critique commenced. Mom's dress—"don't you look pretty... that skirt's a little short for a woman with children unless she's working on Vine street"—or her hair—"Why don't you put some curl to it, such pretty hair going to waste all pulled back." About us, "Lacey, you need to carry Dudley to the dentist, his teeth ain't right. That Lucifer tooth got the devil in it." "The boys' pimples are the result of too much canned food. It ain't good for 'em, Lacey. If you were organized, in the time it takes you to open a can you could shuck fresh corn and cream it on the stove."

Even at the hospital she sniped at Mom. Each of our visits were met with: "These boys need their father's influence so they grow up right. Y'all shouldna never broke up in the first place, and I can only hope you've learned how to be a little more tolerating. You'll have to be if you're ever to get back together again."

Just before her titty surgery she told us she was praying for our dad's return. "Before I leave this earth, I'd like to see ya'll as one family again."

I didn't believe Dad's return had anything to do with Grandma Douglas' digging and bending his will. But her surgery was definitely what brought him back to Cincinnati—according to Grandma. Her cheeks, deflated, barely moved when she said "I'm so glad to see he made it back to see his mother alive, but a course he coulda come home sooner. I coulda died."

Dad would never live it down.

"Mama," he now wiggled up close to her, "you look marvelous."

She looked terrible and funny. On her head sat a high Tina Turner wig. Her dress was noticeably lopsided from her new fake titty.

"Oh Clifton, don't make fun of your poor mama," she sniffled. "This bought tittie is just a mockery."

Dad laughed. "Mom, you look beautiful, and you can buy yourself another titty, one that fits right."

"Don't try to change the subject. If this titty cancer didn't kill me, grief over you would have. As it is, I never see your kids. Lacey never brings 'em by. Not to question the Lord, but why I got to almost die to see my grandkids more regular and for you two to love each other like you supposed to? Somebody tell me why! I'm waiting."

Mom shivered. We had arrived in time for lunch—baked chicken, green beans, and corn pudding. We ate at the dining room table. She had declined Mom's offer of help, and swatted away any comments about conserving her energy. As she moved around the table bringing this and that, it was like staring up at a giant.

"Now, you know, Mother Douglas," Mom defended, "I would have come by a lot more if I had a means to."

"All you had to do was call, and we'd come fetch you. You know this." Then she shouted "Wouldn't we, Cyrus." It somehow never came up that all they needed to do was drive to Finlater, which would have been a whole lot easier for everybody.

"Wouldn't we, Cyrus?" Grandma shouted again, glancing casually at Grandpa for an answer. Grandpa was in the living room, sitting in his plastic-covered mister chair. Grandpa Douglas was a dark little man. His teeth gold-trimmed and hair the color of mushroom soup. He smoked cigars and always seemed on fire. Mom joked he burned cigars to keep Grandma Douglas away. He was hard of hearing after forty years of working at the train yards, and kept the TV loud.

No answer came. Grandma's big knuckled hands shooed Grandpa into the air and continued her point. "'Course, I been telling Lacey all along that it's because of the kids that I wanted ya'll to get back together. It ain't no good for a woman with three boys to be trying to take them to manhood on her own. It's bad enough just trying to feed 'em." She glared at Dad. "And I know you ain't paid her a lick of child support, not a red cent, with your irresponsible ass. I raised him better than that, Lacey, you know I did."

Then her digging aimed at Mom again. "Lacey, why that's a pretty fingernail polish. You know it's unsanitary to keep nails so long…"

Mom looked as miserable as us kids. Fortunately us "grandchilluns"—as Grandpa called us—were excused from the table. We were told to see him for a present. His teeth studying hard on his smoldering cigar, he grinned at us. He pulled his wallet from a back pocket. He could never get our names right, and so didn't try. "You do good in school?" he asked in a blanket-statement way. Corey, Dudley, and I nodded, and he gave us five dollars each, what he usually gave us Christmastime. His vision wasn't too good either. I wondered if he'd made a mistake or had confused today for Christmas.

"Keep it like a Jew."

"What? Grandpa, what did you say?" I was practically shouting. I heard a whine come from Grandma.

"Don't spend it all in one place," Grandpa said, and exhaled a plume of smoke that put a choking end to our chat.

PEoplEs

Señor Santos was our school janitor. He was a brown man, but not like a Nigger. He was from Argentina and had hair like shredded ribbon. He was only a little taller than I was, but he was thick and strong with a neck wider than his head. We had seen him push the big school dumpster. It weighed three-thousand pounds. Sometimes, he would tango with his mop, spinning around in a circle in the bathroom. He had been a chemistry teacher in Buenos Aires, but had to leave his country. He wouldn't tell us why. He said he had children—tres niñas—back home, and I figured he was lonely. Us kids liked to practice Spanish with him. He corrected our accents and pronunciation. Our teacher Mrs. Bluestone vented jealousy—"He should speak Spanish well, it's his language."

He should have had her job. He was nice, especially to the little girls and to us blacks, whereas Mrs. Bluestone always seemed afraid we might touch her. Noah and I would catch him at lunchtime. I usually saw him several times a day. I noticed I hadn't seen him at all this particular day. But with Noah away, I didn't go to the main playground, and I wasn't seeing very clearly—everything a blur. I stayed near the front of school. Winton Road was at the end of the block, and the fields to Noah's favorite place just beyond. Leaving school was an act of truancy. Going to the favorite spot alone would be no fun, so I stared in the direction I was not going to take. For the first time I could remember, I didn't care about school at all, not even to go to the library. I was even going to run off when lunch period ended, something I had never done or even thought about doing before Noah. But I changed my mind, fearing Mom's wrath were I to get caught.

Fortunately, the bell rang and us kids scattered toward class. On my way to government, I saw Señor Santos. He worried down the hall with a cross look. I greeted him, but he pointed at the exit door, shaking his head. I didn't know what he meant until he said "Vamos!"

A half hour later, in Mr. Whittlemore's boring science class, the fire drill bell sounded. Us kids scurried outside again. We organized into our homeroom formations, in lines extending across the playground. Us eighth graders brought up the rear, the fourth graders at the head of the formation. Behind us, at the other end of the playground, kindergarten-through-third-grade kids lined up.

The afternoon was golden and warm, perfect for a fire drill. Me and my sometimes-friend Conrad Baxter caught up. He was telling me about his new Star Trek membership, when the administrators joined us outside, too, all shaking their heads like Señor Santos.

Principal Schor put a megaphone to his lips. "Teachers and students, we have a minor emergency and school is closed. You may not go back inside for your belongings. Please proceed home immediately. If your parents must be contacted, please raise your hand and we will contact them for you. For those of you who cannot go home, please remain on the playground."

Us kids felt like cheering with such joy as only a school closing announcement can bring. Principal Schor cautioned against mischief, adding "Many of you are responsible for yourselves this afternoon. Be the model students that you are."

Delrico found me. "You think the Russians are bombing?"

"Hope not," I said. Only a communist would think such a thing, but we both looked up at the bright sky with total excitement and fear.

It was only one-thirty. Mom didn't get home until three. Normally school let out at three and we were home around four-fifteen. Dudley had a key for just such an emergency.

Our gang gathered, Corey in ecstasy. "I sure wish school got burnt down." Corey's big-foot friend Errol was with us. He wore a size thirteen already.

Dudley and Santiago were too cool for childish expressions. Santiago had a full mustache, while Dudley's was raggedy. He could procure Swedish pussies, and I guess it went to his head. He and Dudley wanted to ditch us, but Dudley's job was to shepherd us kids home. His allowance and a punishment were at stake. Outside the playground, Santiago suggested a different way home. We headed toward Winton Road. I was telling Delrico about Conrad's Star Trek membership, and Delrico said he'd rather join the Soul Train Gang.

We turned onto Winton. We didn't cross it, as Noah and I had, but headed north, toward College Hill. The sidewalk ended abruptly, and our having to walk along the highway scared me, as cars whizzed by. But it wasn't for long. We took steep stairs that led down to a dead-end street. Little white houses were embedded in the hillside. It was all new to me. I didn't know where we were until we came out on King's Run Drive. There was a small farm at the corner, with a narrow glass house for plants. An old tractor rested at the road crossing like a tired, rusted watchdog.

Turning on King's Run Drive would have taken us home. But we kept straight, heading I didn't know where. Dudley and Santiago were in front of us. I asked Delrico if he knew where we were going. Delrico said it was another shortcut home, one that would take us almost right to where I lived. He pointed at the hill and guessed we lived right on the other side of it. "This sure is a long short cut," I said.

We walked past the farmhouse, where chickens pecked the ground. The road climbed up over the property, surrounding it like a neck scarf. As we walked along, the road steepened and turned through woods. I really wondered if we weren't lost.

Delrico was talking about dissecting a frog. Delrico's favorite subject was science, even more than music, it sometimes seemed. He wouldn't hurt a fly, but was curious about dead things. He was telling me about the jars with frogs and hearts and brains in formaldehyde. I'd already seen them before. Delrico was saying there was a baby in a jar.

"The teacher say it was a stillborn."

"What's that mean?"

"Born dead."

"You think it was aborted?"

"What's that?"

I explained about the vacuum cleaner that's put up in a

vagina. Delrico cringed.

A group of black kids were suddenly up ahead. As we got closer, I recognized them from south Finlater. Several cars packed with high hairdos and flailing arms sped past us. They were black kids, only older than us. High-school age. Then I realized we were going to Peoples High School. The school Noah and I weren't attending next year.

The road turned again, but I heard the crowd before I saw it. Hundreds of black kids. School buses smoking on the side of the road, filling with more black kids in one place than I'd ever seen in my life. It was a like a factory at quitting time. We walked through an ever-thickening traffic of bodies and cars. The school was just ahead of us. It was the biggest school I'd ever seen.

"Let's go home," I said, unnerved.

"Naw," Delrico said. "This where you going to school next year, unless y'all move."

"I'm not going to school here," I said.

"I am." He added "eventually."

I heard a scream, popping sounds, and then a car engine gunning. Yelling and crying kids suddenly dove to the side of the road. Then I saw a car charging toward us. It was full of whites. Grown men hanging out the car windows, and shooting. Shooting at us? The oh-shit! fear hit me as I saw Dudley and Santiago dive to the curb, between parked cars. We were far enough behind them that there were no more parked cars, just thick woods beyond the curb. Me, Delrico, Corey, and Errol plunged in. A sound like mosquitoes buzzed in the air as the car sped by us. "Go back to where you come from, Niggers. Africa for Niggers."

The weeds whipped us. We jumped over downed branches and ran faster. Delrico tripped and crashed down a steep hill. I saw him sliding and rolling until he collided with a tree stump.

"Delrico," I shouted.

"Come on, Cliffy," Corey cried.

I glanced back to see if we were being hunted, and then went down the slope after Delrico. He lay there as lifeless as a pile of clothes. His glasses were smashed, his eye bleeding where glass shards had cut him.

I bent over him. I touched his shoulders, called his name, and a fat tear splashed over his dirt-crusted forehead.

"Cliffy."

"Del."

"Cliffy, help me. I can't see."

I looked up the hill and waved for someone to help me. No one did. Corey and Errol had left us behind. I grabbed Delrico's arm and dragged him up the hill. He was completely blind, and so could barely walk, and definitely not run. A few kids ran past us, too. I noticed two girls crying, their bare legs bleeding. All I could say was, "Faster, Del, faster." It didn't matter that I couldn't see danger—I could smell and taste it. Delrico kept muttering, "I'm gonna get killed. My glasses cost a hundred bucks. Grandma ain't got that." I wanted him to shut up.

An embankment led down to a creek. We splashed through

it, then climbed another hill, beating and tripping our way through the thick brush. Finlater finally appeared—not like Dorothy's vision of OZ the first time she saw it, but spectacular all the same, a sight for sore eyes. Blind Delrico must have sensed it.

"We're home," he said.

"Yeah," I beamed, until I noticed the wounded. Bleeding kids cried on the hill. BB-shot wounds dotted their flesh. Corey was among them, with two bleeding dots in his back. "Cliffy," he shouted my name. He was hysterical with fear. He nearly knocked me down, he held me so tight. "It hurts, Cliffy. It hurts."

It was all over the news. Mom was upset. An ambulance carried Mom and Corey to the hospital. The BBs were pulled out of Corey's back. The tetanus shot made him even more hysterical, Mom said. Corey was given a sedative. Poor Delrico. His left eyeball was cut very bad, the sight likely gone for good. He wore a patch as big as a muffin over the bad eye.

Dudley bore the brunt of Mom's anger. No explanation was good enough, and she lit into him. Of course it wasn't his fault that our school had been evacuated because of a gas leak, which Mom found out when she called the school demanding to know why us kids were let loose and nobody attempted to call her. That Dad had been home all along only made her angrier.

"That's why I tell you boys to come straight home from school. You could have been killed. So help me God, we're getting out of Finlater if it's the last thing I ever do."

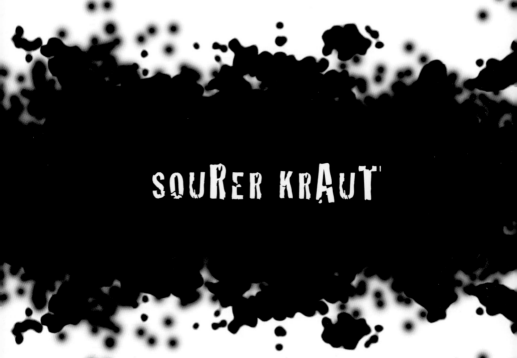

SOURER KRAUT

Mom's overtime was usually one day a week, sometimes two, for a couple hours before or after her normal shift, but never more than four. That was before the Peoples incident. Now she signed up for extra hours every day. That first week, she let us know her weekly paycheck fattened with twelve hours of time-and-a-half pay, and our reward was a full week's worth of Captain Crunch cereal. Tuesday mornings, man-hater Glodine would pick her up at 4:30 A.M., and Thursday evenings Mom rolled in after 9 P.M. One of those evenings, I was pulling groceries from Miss Glodine's car, when the big woman said, "Your mama at least is set on getting you boys out of Finlater before it turns ya'll into criminals."

Miss Glodine hadn't mentioned Dad. I usually ignored her, but now I wanted to say something. I figured she wanted to hear something that would confirm the worst about Dad, not change her opinion, so I said, "Dad, he wants us tough. He don't want no sissy boys."

"Tough," she snapped. "That sounds like something he would say."

"That's what he said," I added. It hit me that if she knew Mom back in high school, even if they weren't friends, she knew Dad, too. She shook her head, the top strands of her new frosted wig swaying like wheat.

"I'm so sick-a-him! And your mama, she ain't got the sense she was born with."

"Huh?"

"You old enough to know this," she said, lowering her voice. I came closer, so close I could see ham or steak in her teeth.

"It's that kind of thinking that got your daddy up in jail in the first place."

"Jail?"

"Trying to be tough. Hanging out with the wrong set. All they did was ride through Amberely Village, where all them rich Jews is—and a course they was planning on a robbery, being the jobless damn fool knuckleheads they were. One of the boys, his mama was a maid to a family there so he put it in their heads to do it for some easy money. Lucky them, they weren't doing nothing except casing when they got busted. You know, when we was young your daddy was very nice—full of he-self like most good-looking men, but not a showoff. Seem like as soon as y'all kids were born, though, he had to show his true worthless colors."

"How long was he in jail?"

"About a week, I think, it was." She cleared her throat, looked around, a little paranoid-seeming. "Scared his black butt enough that all he do now to prove how much a man he is is make kids he don't take care of. Lordy, you'd think your mama woulda been the one to learn, but naw, she had to have him, no matter what. Even back then, after the shot-gun wedding, I told her she'd better not have no more kids by him, and that was after Dudley was born! Did she listen—'course not! He shoulda done her a favor by running off then, instead of waiting until after Corey was born." Then, suddenly lowering her voice, she said—"Glodine, girl, you best keep quiet," as if there were two Glodines present, one with loose lips that needed shushing. "But that, young fella, is between me and you. I'm telling you this now because you cursed with his name, but you ain't got to grow up to be like him."

"I won't, Miss Glodine."

Just then I looked up and spotted Mom standing in the doorway and staring our way. Miss Glodine saw her, too.

"What's a shotgun wedding?"

"Your mama was pregnant and his daddy and your mama's daddy made him do right."

As I ran inside, all I could think of was a vacuum in my mom's vagina sucking Corey out.

"What she say to you?" Mom demanded.

"Nothing."

"That's the worth of anything she got to say."

Mom just confirmed it—what Miss Glodine said must be true, I figured. The first chance I got I slipped a small steak knife into my pocket. As I miserably chewed on a chicken wing, I looked at Mom, at her tired, pretty face, and I wondered why she had to have Dad so bad. What was it about him that made her have us despite everything bad he had done, despite even what she knew, and did she know about abortion? For a second, my obsessive thoughts about Noah came back—how empty and crazy I felt without him. Then I became afraid for all us kids and Mom. If she felt about Dad in anyway like I was feeling about Noah, it could only mean trouble, I figured. Or maybe I had it backwards. Maybe if I felt about Noah the way I thought she felt about Dad, then I was the one in trouble.

"Mom, maybe you shouldn't work so much," I said when we sat down to eat.

"I have to."

"Finlater ain't so bad." I looked to my brothers for a sign of worry or support. Corey and Dudley ate like jackals, gnawing the bones down to nothing.

"You're right, if I... we... didn't want more for you kids." She looked at each of us, to tamp down more criticism. "I'm lucky I got a job that I can work all this overtime." She smiled at me—that worn-out, sad smile. "Don't worry, sweetie, it'll be over soon."

"What will be over soon?" I must have sounded panicked because Corey looked up, rolled his eyes and shook his head.

"The overtime. There won't be any extra work after June. But thank you for the concern, Cliffy." She then glared at my brothers, with what looked like a silently delivered warning that she was in charge and there had better not be any trouble.

So she kept working the crazy hours. Every night she came home late, it seemed to me we were worse off instead of better. I kept thinking that if, as Miss Glodine said, Mom was just stuck on Dad, she was still fifteen-years-old, and yet maybe she was killing herself—not for us but for him—to bring him to her grown-up way of being by example. If Miss Glodine was right, then Mom just couldn't help herself.

But Dad was Dad, and so he couldn't help himself, either. He did just what he wanted, period, no matter what she planned, hoped or wished for. A call from her left him with instructions he usually passed off on us or ignored completely. Us kids knew the drill, but that was not the point. She wanted his participation, to "work together as a unit," as I heard her put it to him. Most times he just didn't bother to come home, his whereabouts unknown.

Poor Mom. I think she took her frustration out on Dudley. Dudley being Dudley, he made himself fair game, though. He nearly always dragged in minutes after Mom. It was a deliberate act of defiance that provoked her. She was still angry at his poor judgment, and he could count on a tongue lashing. "You are not allowed to hang out on the playground past seven, and you know it! You're not as smart or grown as you think." And on and on. I stayed out of her way. I was the least of her worries. I was the one who felt sorry for her. Love could make a person crazy. Crazy enough to do something very crazy.

It was all set, and the showdown came swiftly—so swiftly that I didn't have the chance to run upstairs. That Friday night Dad forgot one time too many to tell us to put leftovers in the oven. He was upstairs on the phone. Neither Dudley nor Corey were at home. Not long after Mom came in he shouted downstairs: "Hey, Lacey, bring me a beer when you come up." She ignored him completely. Minutes later he appeared in dingy pastel bikini briefs. He blazed, "Lacey, didn't you hear me calling you?"

"I'm not your servant, and neither are the boys. I've been working all day, and dammit, I'm tired. Get it yourself. And for godsake, stop parading here in your nasty underwear. It's disgusting."

"So that's how it's gonna be."

Empty Schlitz can in hand, he pounded the steps with bare feet.

It was 9:30 P.M., and I was starved. I was on the couch pretending to reread parts of Stowe, which I had already finished. I was there because I wanted to be close to the phone in case Noah called. I thought I heard her growl "lazy Nigga" but I couldn't be sure. She was speaking into the refrigerator and groping for the leftovers he forgot to warm up. The Teflon pot crash-landed on the stovetop, and it was as if Mom were burning with anger. Her mutterings got coarser and louder until she shouted, "What am I doing all this for? Ask for one simple thing, and he don't do shit. Don't give a damn if his kids run wild, and the Nigger has the nerve to order me around, running around in his nasty drawers with his dick showing."

I was amazed, gripping Stowe. Amazed not at her anger but that it was full of such disgust. Now it seemed Dudley's feelings were justified, and it seemed Mom even shared them. Maybe she had had them all along—but how could she then love him if she hated him so? She came to the living room, turning full on me, as if surprised I was there. She seemed confused, but in an enraged way. I thought she was going to explain away what had just happened. I thought she would ask for my patience and understanding, blaming her exhaustion, worry, hunger—blaming everything but Dad.

"Cliffy, you spying on me?"

"No, ma'am... I was reading my book."

"Yes, you were spying. You were spying on me and your father. We were having a private conversation, and you were spying."

"I wasn't, Mom. I was here before your conversation started..."

"You were spying, that's what I know. Your father says I raised you to be a little punk, and you know, I think he's right. A little busybody, like that Kraut white lady. I shouldn't allow you to do anything else for her."

I couldn't speak. Mom rarely ever raised her voice at me. She was never mean to me. A punk would probably cry right then, so that's what I did.

"Stop acting like a sissy. You're almost fourteen, for pity's sake."

I cried harder. Then, through squinting eyes I saw her hand lift, flex backward into a windup as if she were pushing something away, and then swing out toward my face. Her palm landed just above my ear. WHACK!

"Dammit, stop it."

Her voice sounded as if far away in my ringing, burning ears.

"Stop it," she shouted, lifting her hand again.

And I did. For a few a seconds, anyway, long enough that she lowered her hand and looked away. The anger in her eyes I would forever see, her hand lifting and swinging toward me, and me just standing there, stuck in place, like she had been when that bus nearly hit her and Corey in the snowstorm. The tears blurred her in my eyes and I would never again see her the same.

"I'm sorry." She softened, her fingers pressing to her lips. "Boys need their fathers so they can learn how to act like men. Mothers can't do that, boys need their fathers for that. I need you to grow into a good man."

She shook her head.

I stared down at her white work shoes.

"On my way in, Mrs. Crites told me she hasn't seen you in a while. I told her you'd go over tonight and help her with some problem she's got. While I heat up dinner you go see about the woman before she goes and dies on us."

I turned to leave, as Dad came downstairs again. Bell-bottom jeans gripping his hips, his jean cap at a pimp angle. A uniform slung over his shoulder. He looked at Mom with fist-tight eyes, and she backed toward the sink. He dropped the uniform on a chair, grabbed Mom's shoulder. I ran outside, chased by the plague of their arguing.

I ran to Frau Crites. Her window cranked up and her head craned down.

"Guten Abend, it's Cliffy." I was crying, and unable to hear myself or anything, like I was underwater.

"Liebschen…"

Some German curses followed. The keys sock dropped
heavily. They deflected off my fingertips, landing in the crabgrass.
I ran down the stairs for them. I heard a door slam loudly. Dad
swaggered toward the parking lot, his work uniform choked in his
hand. I didn't want him to see me. I grabbed the sock and hid in
Frau Crites' porch's shadow. The Thunderbird soon roared to life.
Tires screamed as it backed up. Headlights blinked open and
slashed the hill with a blade of headlights. The light cut over me,
unseeing, and the car shrieked into the night.

I hated him. "I ain't no punk," I cried out into the night.
"You're a punk. A megalomaniac." And stupidly I began spelling it,
but I had it all messed up, which for some reason made me cry
even more.

"Was sagst du?" Frau Crites called from her perch in the
window.

I ran up the two flights of stairs. I wished to tell her nothing,
but my face was tear-streaked. A bitterness beat in my heart, and
anger outsized my throat. Her sour-smelling schnitzel churned my
stomach. I was sick. Not even chocolate brownies or cupcakes or
shortbread cookies could make me well. Without Noah, nothing
could make me happy again. Ever.

Frau Crites' own unhappiness was gross. The blubber, the
helplessness, the smelly ulcers. Yet I needed her. I just wanted to
hear her say "Kom hier, liebschen." And to be hugged in her
meringue of a bosom.

JUST DESSERTS

I dreamt I was adopted. The Baumgartens became my parents. Noah and I were together always. We had a big bedroom with bunkbeds, only at night we slept with each other. I ate fried drumsticks and chocolate ice cream for breakfast and got a 10-speed for the A's on my report card. Mr. Baumgarten no longer suffered madness/sadness. He straightened Bikini Dad out with a karate chop to the throat. Bikinis were shed in favor of Hanes briefs. Mom was happy with our newly clad dad. I visited them from time to time. Dudley became a mailman, and Corey a comedian like Richard Pryor. I was a lawyer with a national spelling bee championship under his belt.

A stupid dream.

The Baumgartens didn't return on the weekend. Mrs. Baumgarten didn't call with a new date. I just figured they might be coming back that Monday night for school's sake. But Tuesday morning, when I stopped by, no one was at Noah's house, not even Cupcake. Thursday followed Wednesday, and still no sign. Maybe they were never coming back. Maybe something had happened. Maybe Noah was hurt. Maybe he just forgot about me. I dreamt he didn't care—he'd only been pretending. I couldn't stand it, and I thought about bad things happening to me—broken arm, or leg. A freak tornado touched down in Carthage and tore up everything, killing 16 people. What if I were there, among the dead? Maybe Noah would come home then—but how would I know? I was laughing at my own stupidity, when Mom, sorting the mail, said,

"Cliffy, it's something for you."

It was from Noah. A postcard with a picture of the Empire State Building.

I must have lit up like a Christmas tree because Mom said, "So that's what's been eating you. Worried about your dramatics."

I didn't deny it. I got up to be excused.

"Hey SB, I know you haven't had pizza before, so I put a little on this card plus some of my own special seasoning and if you lick it you can taste it. Wish you could be here because I don't want to come back. Will sneak and call you soon. Your best friend and SB, Noah."

In the bathroom I stared at the spot I knew was his gism. I was happy for a few minutes, just long enough to shoot my own and to realize he might never come home again. There wasn't even a return address for me to write him back. How dumb was that!

I put the postcard in bed with me, mad at him and yet desperate enough to kiss it.

Sunday morning came, and Mom went to work. She told us about overtime, but I forgot and wondered where she was. Dudley headed for Maybelline's coochie, Corey for who knows where. I stayed home. I was afraid of Bikini Dad, but what if Noah called. The phone rang. It was Grandpa Pleasant.

"Cliffy my boy, how are you?"

I always loved that he knew my voice. Nobody else did. I didn't sound like Corey or Mom, but still nobody ever guessed right.

"Y'all getting ready to go to church?"

"No, Grandpa."

"Why?"

"Mom's at work."

"When's she back?"

"Around one."

"Y'all coming to dinner?"

"Probably not."

"Your mom's determined. Working herself so hard."

Grandpa hacked and wheezed. "You tell your mama we're coming out there right after church. We'll be there at two-thirty. We'll be bringing Sunday dinner with us. Tell her we even got sweet potato pie for dessert, so she ain't got nothing to do."

"Okay."

"Take care to let that daddy of your'n know."

"Yes, sir."

"See you soon."

I wrote Mom a note.

Dad called downstairs, "Who the phone for?"

Fuck you!

I slipped the note into my pocket, then myself out the back door. I ran to Delrico's, hoping Grandpa and Dad got into it, and Grandpa wrung Dad's neck.

Miss Tussy said Delrico wasn't home. He was visiting cousins in Kenwood. "Spent the night there, and I 'spect he'll be back tonight."

"Thanks, ma'am. Delrico say I could borrow his bike. Can I get it, please?"

She opened the door. I could see the beast, a blue curvy Sears 3-speed I could hardly lift, in the storage space just beyond the door.

"You mama got $25? 'Cause that's how much it gon cost if you bring it back in pieces, or don't bring it back a-tall."

"I'll take good care of it."

I jumped on the bike, peddling away as she closed the screen door. I rode down to the railroad yard, my favorite place other than the pond. I skipped the stealth route along the back sidewalks of Finlater. Instead, I sped down the sidewalk on the main road, not caring who saw me. I felt like Eliza and Harry running away from bondage. At Estee Avenue, I steered into the street and peddled faster, the heavy bike fighting me all the way. I stopped at the WELCOME TO FINDLATER GARDENS sign which I'd passed by a million times on the bus but had never really noticed before until my spelling bee disaster. Not long after my wipeout, I came down with a can of spray paint and blotted out the "D." It was dusk and it seemed like a million people saw me, but I didn't care, I almost couldn't help myself. I ran home and nobody stopped me.

My vandalism corrective had made me feel better at the time, and seeing the "D" still blotted out felt so cool. Only now NIGGERS was tagged above FINLATER. The sign now read:

Niggers
WELCOME TO FINDLATER GARDENS

I laughed as I rode on. Past Stop 'n Shop, at the southern edge of Finlater, fuel storage containers lined the road like gigantic flour tins. A tall fence with barbwire kept us kids out of the danger area. Mom's old boyfriend Mr. Porter said heating oil for the whole city was stored in them. A careless match could blow south Finlater to Kingdom Come. Mom added "To hell and back." It was clearly the easiest way to get rid of all Finlater, maybe as part of a giant plan to rid the city of Niggers. Kind of like what Noah said about Nazis rounding up the Jews and turning on the gas. Noah would understand. Where was he?

Sunday meant few factory workers, so not many cars were around. I steered clear of the few I saw. One driver yelled, "Fool, get outta the street before you get killed." His bald head was wrinkled like a raisin. I shouted back, "Fuck you."

I veered onto a gravel bed beside the railroad tracks. Trotting over the rocks was easier than peddling. With Delrico, I had snuck down here twice before. The gravel lane narrowed going one way, and widened going the other. Twenty storage tins lined the route I took. The tracks lumbered across a rickety bridge. It looked as if made from Erecto Set pieces, stretching over a pitiful river, not much wider than a faucet stream, and a sickening gray in color. A sign declared it the Buckeye River, not at all what I thought a river looked like. Rivers were as unpredictable as moms and dads.

Beyond it were mountains of coal, the land blackened with dust. A machine straddled cargo containers on the railroad track.

Nobody was around. Up close the rickety bridge was like a jungle gym. Me and Delrico had climbed it before, wedging ourselves onto a platform almost directly under the tracks. We were inspired by a chuffing train coming. The bridge shook and clacked, the sound deafening even with fingers plugging my ears. It was like the massive world was coming to an end, shaking apart, into dust. We clung for dear life for twenty minutes, afterwards covered in dirt. I had almost pissed my pants, and Delrico did piss his. Neither of us admitted how terrified we were. Walking back on the rail bed, we heard a big white man shouting "Get along you little coons. This ain't no toy, you gonna get yourselves kilt." We ran like hell. I loved it there. It felt secret, dangerous, and like an adventure.

Morning had been cool and grey, but rain suddenly fell. It was downpouring by the time I reached the train bridge. I abandoned the bike and sought cover, climbing down the steep embankment. Soon I was soaked through and could hardly see.

The under bridge gave little shelter. The dry spots were closer to its support beams. I squatted, pressing my back against a cement block. I had been there awhile when I heard a moan. It sounded far away. Arriving on the rain-wind like a spinning petal. The moan came again, only this time closer. The hard rain blinded me from a view. It was like staring through a shower curtain, but I could just make out the movements of bodies. Across the river, under the bridge. It looked like two men. One large and down on his knees, the other tall and standing. The moans continued for a spell. Then came a shout, "Pervert, huh, you fat, white motherfucker. Give me your money." The other voice cried, "Take it, only don't hurt me." The bodies struggled, the large one down, while the standing one kicked and punched. Then the standing one ran away from the scene, scrambling up the coal hill.

I hid behind the bridge's foot while my mind raced ahead. The big man down didn't move. I wondered if he was dead. The rain slowed enough for me to see. I had never seen a dead body before. Its shape was like a bowling pin. Its head pointed toward me, bald and pink like Mr. Coursey's. My curiosity wrestled down my fears, the two tumbling back and forth, with no clear winner. I wished Noah were here, or even Delrico. Both were braver than me.

Now the dead man was alive. He lay there flopping like a caught catfish. Hoisting to his feet, he jerked his pants closed, and headed toward me, as wobbly as Frankenstein. Now there was no place to hide, so I ran. Hands clawing and feet digging my way up the embankment.

Delrico's bike was gone. Now I was really in hot water. I headed toward Estee and that's when I saw the familiar car. A sticker in the back window said To Be or Not to Be. It was Mr. Coursey's. That must have been him, I thought. And then, without thinking further, I grabbed a handful of rocks, shoved them into his gas tank, and shouted I SAY FINLATER.

I sprinted home, soaked to the bone, proud of myself over what I had done, and thinking how I couldn't wait to tell Noah. Fortunately, Grandpa Pleasant's car was there. Dad's wasn't. I slipped through the backdoor. Grandma and Mom talked in the kitchen, Grandma at the stove, Mom at the table stirring Kool-Aid.

"Well, here's one of my children," Mom threw her hand to hip. That meant business.

"Hi, Grandma." I ran to kiss her.

"Don't you touch me. You're just like a little wet dog," she said, bending down for a cheek peck. She smelled of roses. Her white-streaked tan hair swirled upward like a Mr. Softee cone. Her pink lipstick left kiss marks she blended away with her thumb. "My my, you getting so big, but then we don't see you no more."

"I hope your brothers are behind you," Mom said. Mom's face looked tight and tired.

"I don't know," I said. "They took off, and I went over to Delrico's."

"I called over there. You weren't there."

"Well Delrico wasn't there, so I went over to Baby Nubs."

"Oh Lacey, let the boy be," Grandma said. "If you weren't working so much all the time, you'd know where your children are."

"Cliffy, you go change into dry clothes."

"Sugar, have one of your Grandma's chocolate chip cookies before you go."

I gobbled one down. Her cookies were as delicious as Frau Crites' brownies. But then I loved everything Grandma made.

The toilet flushed and feet struggled down the steps. It was Grandpa.

"Can't imagine why they didn't put a bathroom on the first

floor. I'm gonna have to carry me a piss jar, shoot."

"Hey Grandpa. I'm all wet."

"What's a little wet? Give your Grandpa a hug."

Grandma was much taller than Grandpa. He was the brown of pipe rust. His hair was white and eyes turning silver like stars in the sky. His eyes used to be light brown, but were changing colors just like his daddy's did. "Yours will too," Mom predicted.

"'Bout time one of you boys showed up. Nobody keeping track of your whereabouts these days, I guess."

"Gene, let the boy go change before he catches his death," Grandma said.

"Look like you grown an inch."

"Maybe."

I ran upstairs. With Dad here, I never went into Mom's room.
I did this time. I pressed my ear against the door. Snoring or TV sounds were absent. I pushed it open.

It smelled strange. Like something burnt. Like bad smelling cigarettes, and really strong. I wondered where Dad's money stash was that was paying for Maybelline's coochie.

I opened drawers, finding only clothes. I opened their closet, finding only more clothes. The nightstand contained bikini drawers on either side. I found a tin box, the kind long ago crammed with Christmas cookies. Now it was full of change—maybe a thousand dollars.

I ran back to our room, my pockets jangly and heavy. I climbed my bed, emptying my loot, spreading my covers over it.

Then I changed my wet clothes.

"Glad you back," said Grandpa. I sat on the couch with him.

"How you doing? I miss seeing you boys, that's why me and your grandma come out today. The way things going, no telling when we get to see you."

He asked about school. I told him about the dramatics.

"Nuttin but white teachers at Elmwood, huh?"

"Yes, sir."

"Figures," he said. "Strange people, them."

"Grandpa, you know anything about Jews?"

"Good people. Don't understand nuddin about their 'ligion, but they good people. Yessir. Terrible what happened to 'em in the last war, owing to Hitler. You know, I was there and saw what them Germans did. Just evil, it was. Like to make me sick, it did. What you wantin to know about Jews fer?"

Should I tell him I was going to be one? No. "Just curious, Grandpa. My friend Noah's Jewish. Father Ferdinand spoke about Jews last Sunday. I figured you'd know."

"Y'all went to church last Sunday, huh?"

"We did," Mom chimed.

Grandpa ignored Mom.

"Well, it's like this, Cliffy, I'd trust a Jew stranger with my life any day before I would a Nigger stranger, that's for sure."

"Dad, don't say things like that to Cliffy, please…" Mom said.

"It's the truth. Only a Nigger will kill you over a keychain. You stick with them Jews and you'll get someplace in life. Times is changing and you'll have opportunity if you get out there and deal with all kinds of people and learn, boy, learn. You stick wid our people and you ain't never gon have shit."

"Gene, you are just terrible." Grandma was standing in between the kitchen and the living room. "Cliffy, come and give Grandma a proper hug."

I did.

"Everything alright, sweetie."

My eyes darted to Mom. Stuff in my head and heart swam around, gushing to get out. I wanted to tell on her—about Dad turning her against us, about being starved until late night, being neglected, being mistreated, smacked, cursed at, lied to, and, yes, Dudley's burn. But with Mom staring at me, I couldn't. Her eyes threatened me. I couldn't say anything.

"Okeydokey." I scratched my ear.

"Really?" Grandma seemed to know better.

"Yes, ma'am." I couldn't look at her.

I didn't have to say anything more. Corey came home, and he was definitely not right. His eyes red as cherries, a stupid grin on his face.

"Hey Grandma," he said, running into her arms.

"Sweetheart." But she pushed him away, her hands gripping his shoulders.

"This child is high," Grandma shouted. "He smells like them funny cigarettes. Mary-jo-juana!"

Mom didn't say a word.

"Damn shame." Grandpa shook his head.

Turned out, the funny cigarettes came from Dad—Corey stole from him, too. Grandpa gave Mom a good tongue lashing. It was meant for the son-in-law he couldn't stand. She admitted it "helps me relax." Grandpa shot back, "...and your kids are turning into drug addicts. And Cliffy, this is what I'm talking about. Get your education, boy, and get way from these no-count Niggers."

I knew the "no-count Niggers" Grandpa was talking about. So did Mom. Grandpa and Grandma scolded, and Mom cried. It was a different cry than her misery one. A pouty, childish cry. Like Dudley's, with his eyes turned down. She agreed to no more smoking that stuff. "It's illegal, Lacey, where's your brain!" There would be a handle on her kids. No more missing church or Sunday dinner.

The no-more I wanted there was still plenty of. Dad, in all his bikini glory, remained, safe in the armor of Mom's love.

Later, Corey got a beating in Dad style, in their bedroom, behind locked door. He screamed as if being killed.

Mom ran upstairs, banging on the door. "You're hurting him."

"That's the point."

She ran outside. She came back when it was over. Silent. Her eyes flooded over when she saw the welts crisscrossing Corey's back. Then her fresh, boiling tears seemed to steam in pain as she tried to comfort him. There was no comforting him.

CoCK & BuLL

Things changed, yet were the same. Corey was now terrified of our dad, yet seemed to love him more. Just like Mom. At night he whimpered in pain, but fell into complete service by day. He ran up and down the stairs at Dad's calling.

Dudley said, "I told you. Look at Corey, acting like a little slave."

We were all Uncle Tom, including defiant Dudley.

Seemed like Mom stayed mad at me. That Grandpa and Grandma's visit was my fault. Or the fact that she didn't know about it was my fault. Which was true. But I hadn't betrayed her to them, and that she seemed to respect. Soon her small touches and kisses resumed, showing she still loved me. But I did not love her—I would never love her again—and so I didn't care. The hurt those nasty words and her slap caused—me the loyal one, me the one bent on her happiness, me who would take care of her always—would never go away. I survived thinking about Mexico, New York, Walnut Hills, and cocksucking. Kissing Noah's postcard. Hugging his words. All things Noah. They carried me as steadily as his bicycle had.

Twenty-four days, and Noah finally returned home. It was a Thursday. Noah's phone call came at dinnertime. Mom told me to keep it short. Since I no longer had a dramatics partner, my phone privileges had been revoked. She gave Dudley and Corey a "don't get any ideas" stare, then loaded a tray for Corey to give Dad.

My heart pounded in my ears. I hoped Mom and my crazy

brothers couldn't hear it. I tried to act cool—"Hey Noah"—but my excitement did cartwheels around the room.

"Hey soul brother. I didn't think we ever were coming back."

"What took so long?" I tried not to sound desperate, to sound okay.

"Stuff happened."

"Why didn't you write your address?"

"Oh, yeah, guess I forgot. Plus I thought we weren't staying."

That was no answer, but I said, "I see."

My back was turned to everyone. I could feel their ears straining for my every word. I saw Mom go upstairs.

"You been reading that book?"

"Yeah."

"Speak up."

"Yeah. I finished it."

"Something the matter?"

Corey mocked me with various kissy-faces, his lips stuck out like a smooching fish.

"My stupid brother's having a seizure. I'll meet you tomorrow morning."

"Early?"

"Cool."

Dudley glared at me. "You and that Jew Honkie. You gonna get your butt kicked hanging around him."

"We got an assignment to do at school. Tell all your stupido friends that."

"Everybody say you an Oreo."

"So?"

"So I can't be having a brother everybody saying bad stuff about."

"I don't hear people saying nice things about your girlfriend. Maybe you should worry about that."

Corey busted out laughing. He squealed like a piglet to make Dudley angrier.

It worked. Dudley sprang from his seat, hulking above the pork chops, and said "Oreo, when they kick your ass don't be surprised if I'm right there with them."

Mom returned and Dudley shut up, his nostrils flared, the raggedy mustache like a smudge.

"What's going on here?" she demanded.

Refereeing was all Mom had left. She didn't know us anymore. None of us volunteered answers. But something in Dudley responded, and her eyes studied him, hard. He wouldn't look at her. His nostrils flared even more, as if to suck her in, then expell her out like snot. I felt the same fury at her, if that is what it was, until she smiled at me, and then I knew different.

"I've got some good news that'll make y'all happy."

I faked a smile of interest.

Corey said, "You got a raise?"

"No."

"You found some money?"

"A quarter on the street, but that's not the news."

Her eyes fell on me. "Cliffy, what's my news?"

A divorce? "I don't know."

"Guess. It's something that'll make ya'll real happy."

Having Noah home made me happy. "You getting your driver's license and getting your own car."

"Yeah, that's true, but that's good news for when summer comes. Guess again."

"We going to Disney Land," Corey said.

"Nope, wrong again. Dudley?"

He shrugged.

"Corey and Cliffy, until your brother takes that hateful look off his face, I'm not going to tell."

"Dud, stop being a dud," smirked Corey.

Dudley crossed his arms. Mom gave up.

"Okay. You'll never guess so I'll tell you."

"We're going to get a house. I applied for this program to help poor folks get houses, and today they interviewed me. They approved my application. We're qualified applicants."

"Wow," I nearly choked. "A house. So we can get a house in Elmwood?"

"Well, if there's one available in Elmwood that's part of the program. See, the houses are city properties that get renovated and sold."

"Remember the house in Elmwood Mrs. Baumgarten told you about?

"I don't know if it's in the program," Mom said.

"I don't want to live with all those white people," Corey said.

Looking at me, Mom said: "It might do you and Dudley some good to hang around more white people. The world's changing. You can't grow up thinking that Finlater is all there is."

She explained the program. The program offered qualified applicants a choice between three or four houses. Each place was selected with the family's size in mind.

She added, "I can ask about the Elmwood house, if you get the address."

"I will."

"Okay. And we'll see."

She petted and kissed me, but it didn't feel the same. Corey stuck his tongue out.

"They already have two places they want us to look at. One is in Walnut Hills, and the other one is College Hill—where your cousins Carmen and Eric live."

"College Hill's cool," Corey beamed.

"Yeah," Mom said. "I like College Hill, too, and it's not far from Elmwood, Cliffy."

"So..." her eyes widened and fluttered. "I need your help. Your father's name isn't on the application. The house is just for us, only your father's part of us."

Dudley's eyes veered up from the table.

"See, I made the application out before he came back. They can't find out he's living with us."

"How they going to find out that?" Corey grinned at Mom.

"They're not. Anybody call here asking for your father, or the man of the house, just say there isn't one or they got the wrong number."

I said, "What would happen if they found out?"

"We wouldn't get a house, or..."

"Or what?"

Her eyes locked on Dudley: "I don't want us thrown out of a house if we're lucky enough to get one."

"And we'd be stuck right here in Finlater," said Corey.

Fibbing was second nature. Lying for Bikini Dad wasn't.

I couldn't sleep that night. Cocksucking dreams teased me. I couldn't wait to feel Noah, to count the hairs above his underwear band. I got up to use the bathroom, to jerk off. The clock said 3:40 A.M. The door to Mom and Dad's room was ajar. No light was on, but moonlight colored their bodies in light like chablis wine. Dad lay on top of the sheet, ankles daintily crossed, his privates lounging on his leg like a sleeping animal. A musty, sour, salty smell was there. I watched, wanting to touch the animal. It stirred. His hand lifted out of the dark, then landed there to pet it. His fingers scratched and rubbed it, in the process pushing it onto his stomach. There, it stretched, reaching past his navel. It began to pulse, lifting. Soon he turned to Mom, rolling onto her, his weight jimmying her legs open. He arched into her. I could see his arms and hands hook under her shoulders. His lips speak into her ear, like he meant to say something but forgot what. His hips drove into her. I watched them, her head shaking as if in pain, or in fever.

She peeked over his shoulder. It was like she couldn't breathe. Or like she were dying except for the sharp gulps of air his weight allowed her between his pushing and pulling. Her struggles egged him on—"give me that pussy, Lacey," he growled. She vanished under his shoulders. Her fingers dug into his back, until she was crying, deeply moaning. Seconds later he said "shit," released her, rolling away from her flattened shiny body. He rolled back to his side of the bed, but not before moonlight caught the wet on his dick, making it glisten like something slithering out of the mud. She rolled against him. Innocent like a child. She looped her arms into his, her hands sliding over his nipples. They rested on his stomach. Like kitty paws.

Us kids didn't matter. This is what Dudley knew. And why he hated our dad, and why our dad burned him, to erase him a little at a time. Us kids didn't matter. We couldn't take her where Dad could. It explained Mom's love, why he could do no wrong. It explained his indifference, why we didn't interest him. She would forgive him everything. She'd believe anything he said. Do all he wanted. Us kids didn't matter. Us kids never mattered. She'd been waiting for Dad's return all along. No other man could win her heart, not even the good ones. Not even the ones who would love us. All along he was coming back. She didn't know when, she only knew that he would. Us kids didn't matter. Us kids couldn't matter. Us kids would never matter.

Soon Mom prepared for work. With quick movements she showered and dressed. The light on the floor beneath my door darkened each time she passed. No more would I be a problem for her. Noah was home, and we would run away. She left and I raced through washing up for school. The window yellowed with the lemon-bright sunrise. I was out the door at six-thirty, running under skies the color of blue jeans.

I watched Noah's house as I neared it. His room must overlook the driveway. He leaned out of the window, making faces with weirdo ears. He vanished, and shortly was standing on the porch as I entered their front yard.

"Hey Cliffy, long time no see." We grabbed each other. Metal twinkling between his smiling lips, wet hair shining like blades of grass.

I could hardly speak my heart beat so fast.

"Well, you don't have to cry about it."

I swiped at my eyes, embarrassed. "I got dust in 'em."

I followed him around back to the garage. Cupcake leapt off the back porch. Her nose approved me, she was as happy as I was that Noah was home. I could see Mrs. Baumgarten's head going back and forth across the window. She seemed to be talking to someone. Noah jumped on the bike. Mrs. Baumgarten shouted through the screen door.

"Noah, I don't want you riding that bike to school until we get a lock."

"Nothing's going to happen to it, Mom."

"That's what you said about the other bike."

"I'll make sure nobody'll take it."

"I don't imagine a bike would be welcome in class. Unless you plan to skip school?" Mrs. Baumgarten's finger pointed at him. "Not only are you not taking that bike, but I'll be getting an attendance report."

Noah let the bike crash to the ground.

"If it's broken, the repair expense will be coming out of your allowance, young man. And good morning, Cliffy, nice to see you again. I'm so sorry we haven't been able to meet your folks, but a lot's happened in our family."

"That's okay, ma'am. I'm very sorry to hear about Mr. Baumgarten's father."

She nodded. "I'm looking forward to meeting your folks soon. Maybe you can come this weekend?"

"I'll ask."

"I hope you've read 'Uncle Tom's Cabin,' because your acting partner hasn't done his homework at all."

"I have," I said.

Noah perked: "I'm almost done, Mom."

"Good. Maybe you and Noah can give the family a little Saturday night preview."

I shrugged. Noah gnashed his teeth.

"I'll call your mom to see if you can spend the weekend with us."

"Mom, can we go?"

I thanked Mrs. Baumgarten. On the way to school, Noah said, "She is so annoying. Always busting my chops."

"What's that mean?"

"It's something we New Yorkers say. It means she's giving me a hard time."

"What for?"

Noah said he and his cousin got into trouble. It was Ari's idea to hit a horse in Central Park with a rock. The horse pulled a buggy with people in it. The panicked animal sprang to its hind legs. Then it bolted off, jumping the curb and running through woods, injuring the passengers, two old ladies. Park police nabbed Noah and Ari.

"It was a pretty sick thing to do, and I don't know why we did it. Well, he did it. I just went along with it. That's the same thing. It was scary watching the horse freak out like that. They're so big."

"What else you do?"

"Not much after that. I got grounded. We skateboarded, played basketball, we went to a Knicks game, we went to Coney Island. I had a good time. It's so much better than here. So much to do."

"What about the funeral?"

"That wasn't fun."

"Maybe we should runaway to New York and skip Mexico?"

"Maybe. Only I have so much family there already, seems like it would be counterproductive."

"Okay."

"Maybe Ari can run away with us."

I found myself hating Ari. "Did you and Ari milk it?"

"Yeah." He grinned again. "Only it wasn't much fun because his is real tiny, like an eraser head. Maybe they cut it off during his bris."

"What's that?"

"It's when the extra skin gets cut off your dick. You know, circumcision. It's a religious thing Jews do and make a party out of it. It's pretty stupid."

"I did it with Delrico. And his was really big, only it had that skin over the top still." I nearly added my dad had the same kind of skin on his, but he wasn't worth our consideration.

"I'd like to see it. I wouldn't put my mouth on it though. Not an uncircumcised one. Maybe he'll do it with us sometime. Hey, maybe we can give him a bris."

"Maybe," I said. I was disgusted. I did it with Delrico to get him off my back. Three's a crowd. Maybe if Ari ran away with us, Delrico could, too. That way, he would have his own Nigger, except Delrico didn't like Jews.

"How's your dad?"

"He's in New York... I didn't see him."

"How come?"

"I just didn't. Mom says he's better. All I know is I've got two quizzes to make up."

School waited just ahead. Kids frenzied on the playground before the school bell rang. I told Noah about Mom's house application approval, explaining what I knew about the process. Maybe there were Elmwood houses in the program.

"My mom probably knows." He looked down at the ground. "Maybe my dad'll be home soon. Maybe him and your dad can fix the house up."

I said maybe and left it at that.

Mr. Coursey applauded Noah's return. He himself had been out a few days the previous week. The school secretary told us kids he had had the Chinese chicken flu, and his substitute, a Mr. Blaylock, was so boring I actually missed Mr. Coursey. Our reviled teacher returned with no fever or cough that I could see, but his eye was blackened and his left arm in a sling. He told us kids he'd been in a car crash with an intoxicated colleague from his university days behind the wheel. "I know you are just urchins, but as your teacher I must warn you never to drive with liquor in your blood. A terrible, possibly lethal mix indeed. It's just as well that you know now, because goodness knows the thirst is frequently acquired at a young age."

His misfortunes made him empathetic. He said his attitude— "the show must go on"—changed with his scabs and bruises. His accident had happened the second week Noah was away. He granted me a full week's reprieve. He said "We'll put your performance off until the 20th of May, and hopefully your partner will have returned. But if he doesn't..."

His misfortunes didn't give me—his so-called "best student"—empathy at all. At lunch I sneaked over to the parking lot to find his car. Surprise: there it was, crashed up just like he said. I figured the rocks would have busted his engine up, but I guess not. Maybe I messed somebody else's car up, but I had been so sure—how many cars quoted Shakespeare in the window? I felt a little sick at the thought and feared I was becoming a juvenile delinquent. But like my spelling bee flop, done is done.

Now Mr. Coursey grinned as Noah took his seat, trilling his good hand's hairy fingertips together with the slinged-up ones.

"Mr. Baumgarten, so good of you to come back to the cast. Mr. Douglas, aren't you thrilled?"

"Yes, sir," I said.

"We shall be a captive audience for you the Monday coming, isn't that correct, Mr. Baumgarten?"

"Yes, Mr. Coursey."

"You mother assured me you were abreast of your assignment."

The class snickered.

"Children, abreast means informed," Mr. Coursey huffed.

"Have you kept abreast, Mr. Baumgarten?"

"Abreast I am, Mr. Coursey."

"Very well then," he smiled. "I have a piece of advice, or direction as they say in the theater. And that is, once you've learned your material, go with your gut. You, Mr. Douglas, must find your inner slave, and the dread and pain of the chains that your forebears felt, and Mr. Baumgarten, as I don't know what passage you two have selected, you must tap into similar inner reserves of fear, cruelty, and outrage. You must know that a terrible past stirs in your blood, too. We suspect who Mr. Douglas will play, but my hope is that you, Mr. Baumgarten, will be an interesting Simon Legree—and for inspiration, you need only pretend he is Palestinian."

Noah looked like he was about to kill Mr. Coursey. But Mr. Coursey had moved on.

"I'm so excited that our school year will end on an inspiring note. Now class, I believe Miss Shoemaker and Miss Fargo are to recite poetry by a Daughter of the Confederacy."

On the playground, Noah said, "I hate that fat, racist, anti-Semite motherfucker."

"I hate him, too. Mr. Dandruff."

"We should report him to the principal. I gonna tell my dad. We'll get him fired."

"Yeah, let's do that. What did he mean by 'pretend he's a Palestinian?'"

"Palestinians hate Jews, like I said before—my Uncle Ben, remember?—and that's why we hate them."

"Like the Klan hates black people?"

Noah nodded with a kind of wobbly certainty.

"Why?"

"Israel."

"I don't understand."

"It's our land, but they want it back."

"So it was theirs?"

"It was ours, only they had it, they ran us off hundreds of years ago. We got it back at the end of World War II. The United Nations helped us take it."

"And, the Palestinians... is that why they killed your Uncle Ben..."

He cut me off: "They killed him because they hate Jews."

"Oh," I said. But I didn't understand. It was so confusing. Niggers didn't have nothing but black skin to inspire a history of horror.

"…and everybody hates us."

"I don't, Noah," I said, surprised at how upset he was. "I don't hate you. I'll never hate you."

"Of course, not you, SB." He smiled, his hand brushing mine. "And what happened to Mr. Piggy Shakespeare anyway?"

"He said he was in a car crash. He looked so pitiful last week. His eye all purple and swollen, like he had a jelly Danish over it."

"He was probably eating one when he crashed." Noah laughed. "I wonder if anybody that fat has a dick."

"No telling. But he's got to pee somehow."

"Maybe he has a vagina?"

"That's what his eye looked like. A vagina."

We doubled over, our arms locked or hands pushing each other's away. The sun lit the silver of his teeth. Food scum and small bright lip scabs didn't mar his mouth's beauty.

I then told Noah about the black man beating up the white man in the railroad yard. I waited a few moments before adding, almost as an afterthought, that I thought it was our swine teacher.

"But what would he being doing down there?"

"I don't know. He was on his knees, pleading for the guy not to hurt him. The guy hurt him anyway."

"Maybe he was sucking the guy's dick. Think about it."

"What?" It hadn't crossed my mind.

"He's a big nelly. You can tell."

"How?"

"Look at him, they way he talks and stuff. See, when you get old and act like that you're a faggot. Me and you, we're just kids. Soon as we start getting pussy, it'll all change."

"Oh." I thought of the pussies I knew: Maybelline, Chanel, and the Swedish lady. Nothing! I was going to hell, definitely.

"What if it doesn't change?"

"It'll change."

"How do you know?"

"Trust me. We're not limp-wristed queers. I'm tough. So are you?"

"Maybe Mr. Coursey was just like us when he was a kid?"

"Oh, come on! Look at him. Shakespeare. His Elizabethans. The pig."

As if being obese and liking The Bard proved anything. I realized Noah didn't know what he was talking about at all. I was scared. Would I always be this way—grossed out at the sight of pussies? Maybe I just needed a nice pretty girl's to be happy.

Was I tough? Was vandalism an act of toughness or stupidity?

I changed the subject from coochies to criminality.

"I put rocks in Mr. Coursey's gas tank."

"Wow, get outta here! I'm proud of you," he said, laughing. "SB, honestly, I didn't think you had it in you."

"Guess you don't know me half as good as you think, huh?"

"Guess not."

I nodded. I told him about us kids getting shot at Peoples, and about the hole in Corey's back.

"SB, if we're going to run away, we should do it soon, before school's out. Maybe right after I spend Saturday night at your place, we could take off. You think?"

"What's the rush?"

"I thought you wanted to—that's what you said before you went to New York?"

"I'm game, but you don't just run away. You have to make a plan."

"What you mean, make a plan? Like call a travel agent or what?"

"We can't take off with nothing. What have we got?"

"I've got money."

"How much?"

"I don't know, a whole bunch of quarters, nickels and dimes." It was probably twenty dollars but for some reason I said two hundred dollars.

"Cool, that's more than I got in my savings account. Hey, I got one of those coin-rolling machines. Bring your money with you tomorrow."

He stared toward the end of the playground. He looked at me and there was a weird smile on his face. He then pointed at a girl with a blond kinky Afro.

"See that chic, you know her?"

"No."

"Her name's Jasmine Wanamaker. She's a fox."

My mouth must have dropped open. He waved to her, she waved back.

"I like her. Her mom's friends with my mine. They came by last night. I felt her tits up."

I didn't feel so good. My throat soured. A second later I threw-up.

"Ugh, gross." Noah said, jumping away. "What's the matter?"

"I feel sick."

"Probably those nasty cafeteria fish sticks."

I threw up some more.

"Gee, maybe you should go to the hospital or something."

"No, I'm okay."

It passed after a few minutes. I could see Delrico at the playground's edge, waiting, with his muffin eye bandage. Lucky me, he was so happy that I helped him that he wasn't pissed about the bike since he couldn't see to ride it no-how. He told Miss Tussy that the same men who shot us were still around, and they stole it.

She believed him.

"Damn, soul brother, I gotta go round up my sister and brother. You got a sleeping bag?"

"No."

"What about a knapsack?"

"No."

"No bike, no knapsack, no sleeping bag. To run away proper, you need all that stuff." His eyes seemed to scold. "Don't y'all have anything?"

I shrugged.

"It's because you're poor."

I looked away as my throat soured again. I wanted to vomit, cry, and hit him all at the same time.

"I'm sorry. I didn't meant that. It ain't your fault."

"No, it ain't."

"I should've figured out that's why ya'll didn't buy clothes at Ben's, why you don't have a bike or anything, and why you live in Finlater."

"Someday I will have things, a house, my own car, a bunch of money. I'll have everything, even more than you'll have," I swore. "When I'm grown-up, you'll see."

"SB, I know, I know." He touched my shoulder. "Not to sound like a pussy, but, truth is, the reason it took me so long with that book is that it really bothered me. I just don't get it. It made me so mad and so sad." He shook his head. "I better go. Bring your money and we'll start rolling. How about you come at eleven? That way we can ride around and have some fun before we start our 'theatrics.' Man, what a nelly that Mr. Coursey is."

"Yeah." He moved toward the white girl.

I didn't throw up, I ran home instead. The urge to run was as outside of my control as the need to vomit. A fever without temperature burned in me. Soon I was drenched in sweat.

The last person I wanted to see was Dad. I wasn't as afraid of him now, probably only because I hated him so much. He was standing at the kitchen sink. He was shirtless. A tuft of black hair smack in the middle of his broad chest was slick with sweat. His nipples stuck out like candlewicks. He was washing out one of his slinky shirts. He wrung it free of water, twisting it in his hands.

"Hey Cliffy, how you doing?" A can of Schlitz was on the table.

"Fine." I made my way through the kitchen.

"Hold on there, boy."

Usually he wanted something from the icebox brought upstairs. Seldom did our service go in the other direction.

"Why you all sweaty?"

"I ran home."

"You looking pretty sad? All heartbroken. You in love or something?"

In love? That's what's wrong with me? I shook my head no. "I threw up."

"Shit, at least you ain't pregnant like some people I know."

"Boys can't…"

"What you need is a little bicarbonate. Wait right there."

He put the shirt on a hanger. He wanted me to hold it over the oven so it could dry. I stood there with it, as the hot air set my skin to broiling. He went to the cupboard. He spooned some white powder into a glass of 7Up. "Drink this."

I drank it. It was sweet and awful. I belched fast and sloppy.

My head began to drum, loud.

He seemed to find my belch funny, as he waved his shirt rapidly back and forth over oven heat.

"See. That shit works every time."

"Thanks."

"You probably got a nervous stomach like me. I used to play football in high school, when I met your mom. She probably told you that. I played tight-end. Just before the game, I'd go right to the bathroom and throw up like a pregnant bitch. Fine after that."

I nodded. "May I be excused?"

"Just a sec…" He smiled. "I hear you gonna be staying with those Jews this weekend."

"The Baumgartens."

"They all got names like that. Some whities talk a good game, but they don't mean shit. Them Jews, they whities, don't forget, and you gotta watch 'em. I'll grant you, times is changing, but boy, the shit I've seen. They had to pass a goddamn law so we could drink out of a public water fountain, or even go take a shit in a public bathroom we pay taxes for. Your ass was sick, you might as well die because ain't no hospital was gonna see you no how. Don't for a minute think I'm sorting mail at the post office 'cause I want to. Oh no, stupid I ain't. I went to college out there in L.A., sure did. Got an associates degree. Know what that is?"

I shook my head no.

"It's a college education, or half of one depending on how you wanna look at it. And I did it on my own, too, in bookkeeping.

I did it because I could do that in Cally. I felt free there. Shit, there's more Mexicans than us so they leave a black man alone. If it weren't for my mama's cancer"—he looked around, lip curled with disgust—"well, shit, I don't even know why I came back."

"Maybe you should go back, since you were free."

"Yeah," he grinned. He waved the shirt back and forth over the oven mouth. "Maybe I will. One day. Maybe when my mama kick the bucket—and I get some inheritance. That cancer is some serious business."

"She gonna die?"

"Yeah, well, that's what they said but she still here," he said, sounding disappointed. There was also a funny look in his eyes. It was hard to imagine him, or anyone for that matter, being attached to drive-you-crazy Grandma Douglas, so I guessed it was about the inheritance, but then he threw me: "You only got one mama, boy. Remember that."

"I will."

"And you watch yourself with them Jews."

Right then the Baumgartens meant more to me than Mom or the Douglases. I wanted to know if he was talking doo doo.

"Jews do something to you?"

"Yeah, the shysters sold my jewelry in pawn knowing I was coming back for it, and you go down to that ponykeg and look at them Jew prices. Jewing us left and right. Shit, if they owned this place, it'd be a ghetto by now."

"Mom says it is a ghetto. And Mr. Baumgarten, he marched on Washington and bussed down to the South as a Freedom Fighter."

"Did he now?"

"…and he got his hands blown up in Vietnam. And Mrs. Baumgarten, she's a lawyer. She helps poor women. She's what's called a feminist."

"She got a mustache or something?"

"No."

"Them feminist usually be dykes. You know what that is?"

"No."

"It's a woman that likes pussy. Like Glodine, that big ugly bitch, since way back in high school, she was in love with your mama."

Miss Glodine! He could say anything he wanted about her, but nothing he could say could taint Mrs. Baumgarten.

He scowled. "Nice or not, you just be careful round them people. Something go missing around there, they all be crying Nigger."

I turned to go.

"And the next time I wave to you, you wave back."

"Huh?"

"That day I saw you flying on a bicycle."

I sheepishly looked away.

"Didn't you see me waving at you?"

"No."

"You didn't see me at all?"

I shook my head no. "I would have waved, Dad."

He admired his shirt and his "ironing technique." He toweled the sweat from his chest and underarms and slid into the shirt, careful to touch it with fingertips only. He swallowed the Schlitz. He told me to tell Mom he had to go, he'd be back a little later.

I watched him strut away, feeling vomitty again. Dowdy white ladies in the parking lot struggled with grocery bags. They were plain and plump and old, and by contrast Dad looked as if he was from another planet. I wondered what "Cally" was like, and if everybody, the Mexicans included, dressed and acted like him. I decided I hated "Cally."

I climbed to my bed and slept.

It was Mom's voice that woke me.

She jostled my arm. "Cliffy, honey, what's wrong? You feeling okay?"

"I threw up."

"Can you get down?"

I did and we sat on Corey's cot.

The back of her hand took my temperature.

"I been doing a little of that myself. I'm sure you don't have my problem." She kissed me. "You don't have a fever. Probably some bad food."

"It was fish sticks. I feel okay now."

"Maybe you should spend the weekend home."

"No," I jumped up. "There's nothing wrong with me."

"You detemined to be with those people, huh. Where're your brothers?"

"Guess they're not home from school yet."

She shook her head, then looked around, as if in search of something. "Your father was here when you came home?"

"Yes, ma'am. He told me to tell you he'd be back."

"Oh," she said.

"I fell asleep. Sorry."

"No, sweetie." Her fingers brushed against my cheek. She got up to leave. "Don't sleep anymore or you won't be able to sleep tonight."

"Yes, ma'am."

"Dinner'll be ready soon. Come down and keep me company if you want."

I didn't say anything.

"By the way, do you remember if your friend's mother is coming by here to pick you up at ten or eleven tomorrow morning?"

"She's not coming by here."

"Yes, she is. I told her I didn't want you going up to Elmwood by yourself, especially after what happened at Peoples. She was away and didn't know about it, but she understands exactly how I feel. She's coming by to get you. I think she said eleven."

"No, I don't want 'em to come here."

"But you're…"

"No, call and tell her no, Mom. Noah and me will meet up at

the park entrance. We've done it before. I'll be fine. I'll call her myself."

Mom waited at the door of lies I'd been telling. But she didn't push it open. Mrs. Baumgarten must not have given me away. Mom's look was pained.

"Cliffy, you have nothing to be ashamed of."

I was ashamed. I was ashamed of Dad, of Finlater, of not having a bike, a sleeping bag, a house. I was ashamed of everything—including her.

Just then I seemed to be the source of her shame.

"I guess you won't be going then," she said.

"No, Mom, I'm not ashamed. Me and Noah already planned it. He's meeting me in the park at eleven."

She shook her head.

"I don't want to get an F in Mr. Coursey's class."

Still shaking her head, she said, "Cliffy, you getting an F and Mrs. Baumgarden coming to pick you up have nothing to do with each other."

I was mad. "It's BaumgarTEN."

Mom left shaking her head. I lay there. I wanted to run away right then. I never wanted to see Finlater again.

Not long after, she stuck her head in the doorway. "Noah and his mom will be picking you up at eleven, and on Sunday your father and me will be picking you up after I get back from Grandpa's. We'll figure out the time later."

"Mom."

"That's how it is, Cliffy. You don't like it, keep your little smart-aleck butt right here."

She pulled the door closed, but opened it again.

"One last thing. The only thing you should be ashamed of is the fact that you're ashamed. We don't choose our families or our families' situations. Hopefully you'll do better in your life than I have. You'll have a big house, a fancy car, and a family acceptable to the friends that you choose to have."

"Bitch," I hissed under my breath as she banged the door behind her.

Overnight, Mom must have got it. Six loads of wash started cycling at the crack of dawn. Us kids had to complete our chores by ten-thirty. The house was Spic & Span clean and smelling like Glade's Garden of Eden scent. There was no coincidence in Mom's wearing pancake and lipstick and her eyes done up. By eleven her nerves must have caved completely. She insisted I have my overnight stuff ready at the door. When Mrs. Baumgarten arrived, fifteen minutes late, Mom shouted upstairs that they were here. I was to come down to the parking lot at once.

From my post in the bathroom, I also saw the Baumgarten's station wagon pull up. I saw Noah, Leeza, and Isaac and Mrs. Baumgarten set upon by Mom, who was waving like she was trying to flag down a bus to send it in another direction. They hadn't even closed their car doors yet.

I ran downstairs for my suitcase. I was out the door on Mom's heels. I arrived just as she was shaking Mrs. Baumgarten's hand. Mom looked as if she weren't breathing as she explained what a mess the house was. "You know how it is with children when you work."

"Do I! I'm a housewife and I still can't keep a clean house. I haven't seen the bottom of the kitchen sink in years." Mrs. Baumgarten giggled. She held Mom's hand like an old dear friend. And it seemed as if they did know each other. They smiled so much at each other they were giddy.

Mrs. Baumgarten said, "I thought your name was familiar

and I should have known. Cliffy looks just like you."

Mom looked at me. "Well, he does, doesn't he?" She seemed uncomfortable. "That was a bad time. I don't remember anything."

"Some things it's best not to forget." She squeezed Mom's hand again. Mrs. Baumgarten looked at me and Mom seemed embarrassed. "And what a delightful boy you have here."

They knew each other, but how?

I forgot about them. As Leeza and Isaac clung to their mom, Noah gave me a guy's shove.

"Which door is to your house?" he asked.

"That one, second on the right."

There was nothing to see. He wandered up the flight of steps as if he were going for a look around. I could see Mom's eyes blink in my direction. And I noticed Frau Crites peering out her kitchen window. I didn't wave, her being German and them being Jews.

I didn't follow Noah, so he came back.

"I was talking to Ari, and his mom said he could come visit soon as school's out. Ain't that cool?"

"Yeah," I whispered, "if we're still around."

"Huh?"

"Me and you, hit the road. Vamoose. Skedaddle."

"Oh yeah," he said.

Domestic matters gave Mom and Mrs. Baumgarten an even more visible bond.

"...or the time my youngest helped me out by washing the dishes in vegetable oil," Mom said. Mrs. Baumgarten responded,

"Just be glad you don't have a dog to add to your miseries. Dirt and wet-dog smell aren't even the worst of it. Our Cupcake poots all the time. You'd never think dog food could produce a smell like that. It just turns your stomach. It's gotten so bad we keep a box of wooden matches in every room of the house. Noah there struck one a little too close to Cupcake's behind, and poof. I've never seen that old dog move so fast."

Mom's laughter rolled. One hand nearly covered her mouth while the other clutched just under her breast. She rocked back and forth as if in pain. Mrs. Baumgarten's laugh itself egged Mom on. It was a kind of whiny.

Noah and I looked at each other, and shook our heads. I wondered if he hated his mom as much as I hated mine.

"SB, you really do look just like your mom. I look like my dad."

"No, you don't. You look like Scooby Doo."

"Guys," Mrs. Baumgarten said. "We should go. Leeza here has a tap class this afternoon, and we have groceries to get."

"It's so nice of you to pick Cliffy up," Mom said.

"I can use the extra hands, and you can bet he'll earn his keep this weekend."

Us kids piled into the car. Noah and me into the part of the station wagon where the seats faced backward. He was talking to me, but I heard Mrs. Baumgarten say, "It really is so nice to see you again, and to find you so much better. If you ever need anything, call."

"Thank you. Soon as my husband's home from work, I'll let you know about picking Cliffy up tomorrow."

Mrs. Baumgarten climbed into the car. "We can drop him off if it's a problem."

"You're too nice. I'll call later. Thanks again."

Mom blew a kiss to me as the car pulled away. I ignored her. Noah was showing me a pocket watch he found. As we started down the main road, I noticed the Thunderbird as it just passed us, its rear turn signal in a cascade of red light.

"That's a cool car?" Noah said.

"Junk."

"Pimp-mobile."

"Junk pimp-mobile."

Mrs. Baumgarten, with her strawberry cheeks, dropped us off with a threat. "You two had better behave yourselves. It's not you Cliffy, it's him I am suspicious of."

I hadn't been beyond the kitchen before. Mrs. Baumgarten wasn't kidding when she said the house was a mess. Clothes, books, dolls, comic books, coloring books, toys, games, and old dirty dishes spilled out of the kitchen into every room. Noah's was the messiest so far. The floor was somewhere beneath dirty clothes, schoolbooks, notebooks, and God knows what. Liking and being used to order as I was, I was pretty grossed out, but it was so cool that his mom didn't care.

"That's your bed over there."

"Over where?"

He swept the clothes covering the mattress to the floor.

He tackled me and we wrestled around in the laundry heap.

"I'm hard already. You?"

"Yeah."

He slid out of his pants and underwear. I did, too. We wrestled again, twisting and grabbing and pulling. Our foreheads ground into each other's, and our dicks wedged between sweaty stomachs. My lips were smeared with the salt on his neck and arms. My arms got pinned down, his face just above mine, a wisp of spit swinging from his mouth, like a growing thread of silk, his sweat splashing onto my face, into my eyes, blinding me.

"Turn over," he said.

I did and he lay on me, our bodies squishing with sweat.

"Can I put it in you?"

I didn't know what he meant, but I figured it was like putting it in my mouth. "Okay," I said.

"It's gonna hurt at first. Just bite down real hard on your finger."

"Okay."

He spat and pushed, and when it began to feel like I was being stabbed I threw him off me.

"That doesn't feel good."

"Not at first. But then it does."

"You done it before?"

"Yeah."

"With Ari?"

"No."

"Who?"

"You let me, and I'll tell you a secret."

I gritted my teeth and curled my toes. He spat and pushed again. It didn't hurt less, but more. He licked and breathed in my ear as he pushed and pushed. How could it be that he was trying to hurt me, with his breath in my ear, soothing and calming. I thought of my mom, my dad between her legs, and I wondered if this is what she felt, this hard hurt between her legs. But she cried not from pain but from something else, something that allowed him to control her enough to have his way. I pushed him away and lay down on my back. "Let's do it this way," I said. We fumbled around and I lifted my legs as Mom had done. He pushed and it went in. That's when I knew what Mom knew, as I stared into his sweaty red face, the hair swinging over his eyes. I wanted his face to meet mine, our lips to press against each other. We grinded and bumped until we burned and shook. His arms relaxed and he lay on top of me, his head lowering and lips brushing the side of my face as his head wedged beside mine. "Wow," he said. "It was never like that before." He rolled off onto his side.

We lay there staring at each other. My fingers drew the hair plastered on his cheek away.

"Did you like it?" he asked, his eyes closed.

"Yeah," I said. But my butt burned and I wondered if my guts would fall out.

"Oh," he seemed surprised. "I told you. Why don't you do me

now?"

I did, only he didn't like it. We tried and tried. His face drew up in a knot and I felt like I was killing him. I wanted to see his face light up and yield to mine, as I had to him, as Mom had to Dad. "Give it to me, Noah," I said. He tried. My dick head pushed into him and he let out a yelp that unnerved me. Finally, we just ended up wrestling, with me rubbing against him. He liked that more. He offered: "That feels better. Maybe my hole's too small."

"Your mouth isn't, though."

He laughed, and put his mouth there until the trembling ended.

We lay still, our bodies entangled. The next time we folded together, the hurt was brief and sharp, giving way to a desire to envelop him. Our eyes didn't finally meet until we were through. He smiled down at me, but I reached up and pulled his face to mine. He hesitated as if unsure. Then our lips met. "SB," I whispered, giving more to him. The energy squirted out of me again. I could feel it splashing on my stomach as he did the same, only inside me, and I felt it.

"Hot damn," he said. Then he laughed.

"What's funny?"

"Well, I can't believe we did all that."

"I thought you did it before. You're the pro."

"Not like that," he said. I pulled his face to mine and we kissed again. "It never felt like that. I never did all we did. I never kissed like we kiss."

"What did it feel like?"

"It felt okay, but..." The usual mischief in his eyes vanished. I rolled up beside him. "Well, I... alright soul brother, swear on your life you'll never tell."

I did.

"I had this friend Hector. Me and Hector used to horse around like me and you do, only not like what we just did, or at least not the way we did it. Hector was my first. He knew all kinds of stuff kids around here don't. He was so cool. One Saturday I spent the night at his house and I woke with my dick in his mouth. After that, he liked me to stick it in his butt, only he'd bite a sock and he had big bleeding pimples on his back. He wasn't beautiful like you, and we were guys just messing around. Anyway, you maybe seen him before but not this year or last year because he went to Roger Bacon. He had some guy on the football team doing him. Guess I wasn't good enough. Last summer his family moved to Texas. Anyway, so one night Hector was over and my dad walked in on us sucking each other off. Guess I forgot to lock the door."

"Wow."

"He didn't go screwball on me or anything like that. My mom's square but my dad's so cool, you just don't know how cool he really is. I didn't know how he would take it, but I figured he'd be really mad. But all he said was that I couldn't bring Hector by the house any more under the circumstances. 'But in no way am I saying you shouldn't like or love Hector,' that's what he said. Can you believe it? He's done all kinds of stuff and been around the world, so I wondered if maybe he used to have a friend like Hector when he was my age. Right? But who talks about blowjobs and cornholing with their dad? Right? I didn't say anything then, but it was in the back of my mind and then... Okay, so I told you how he gets so depressed. And you know what it's been like with him lately. It was Yom Kippur—a Jew holiday—and everybody went to synagogue but me and him. I had pretended like I was sick and Mom, being worried about Dad, didn't make me go. I had been out riding my bike and I came home and found him sitting in the basement alone, crying. I swear, Cliffy, something just snapped in me. I just couldn't stand seeing him like that. It was like I wanted to help him so bad that I wanted to hurt him, and I even hated him, just then, because I felt so bad. So I begged him to let me help. Anything, I kept saying, anything. So he..."

"He what?"

"...I didn't know what he wanted me to do. First he asked me to tell him about Hector. You know, what me and Hector did. What it felt like and stuff like that. Then he asked me if me and Hector cornholed each other. So I asked him if he had a friend like Hector. He said he did. His friend was a Dominican named Julio, and they were sixteen. He said he loved him. He loved him the way a boy loves a girl. He asked me if I loved Hector like that. I told him no, it was just fun. I asked what him and Julio did. They did everything and they kissed each other and stuff. I asked him if his dad caught him like he caught me. He shook his head no, but his mom found a letter Julio wrote, and my grandpa sent Dad off to a mental institution in upstate New York. And they kept him there, locked up. Can you believe it! My grandpa called Julio's folks, and Julio got kicked out of the house. They threw him to the streets like a dog. Dad was released about a year after they put him there, and he met a girl he also loved, he said. My dad went to music school in the city and this girl was going to college in the city, too. He said he was visiting her on campus one day and he was waiting for her in a park—Washington Square Park, he said. He noticed a group of homos, some of them dressed in women's clothes and they were all talking very loud and acting ridiculous and retarded. He said he watched them for a minute or so, then ignored them. But soon a man came up to him. Dad said he was skinny, kind of grimy and sick-looking, with sores on his face, like a heroin addict. 'Noah, you come for me?' the strange man said. Dad said it took a few minutes before he recognized Julio. 'You come for your Julio?' he said again. My dad said he just panicked. He ran away in the other direction, as fast he could. He felt so bad."

"He didn't go back for him, to try to find him again?"

"No, he just ran away. He said he never went back to look for him or anything because he was afraid, he said. Afraid he'd be put back in the institution. He said bad things happened to him there, so bad he wouldn't even tell me. He was terrified his dad would send him back."

I selfishly thought of myself. Was Julio's fate mine if Noah and me were discovered by my family?

"My dad was crying even as he was telling me about it. I really love my dad, and I wanted to help him. You don't know how awful it is when he's like this. You can't breathe, and we all get sad, even Cupcake. And now that I knew what was making him so sad—leaving Julio on the street like that—I just thought I'd do anything to make him better. I just thought about how good I feel when you suck me off, and I…"

I looked away.

"I asked if it would make him feel better if I pretended to be Julio. He looked shocked. Then he said, 'It's judgment day, so what the hell, I'll have something to really atone for.' Soul brother, I swear it only happened that one time. I was only trying to help him. I swear—and he really only touched me, before he completely freaked out. He was crying and begging me to forgive him. 'I'm so sorry, Noah, Oh God, forgive me…' Over and over he said it. Cliffy, he's in a psycho ward again. They hook him up and zap him with electricity, just like before. That's the real reason we stayed in New York."

We lay there, quiet.

"He's not coming out. He's really gone this time." Noah rolled his eyes backwards until they were whites. "I know it's not my fault."

I wanted him to be quiet.

"It wasn't wrong what I did?" His eyes puddled.

"Noah, if I had a dad I loved like you do yours, I would have done just what you did."

"You would?" His eyes were full of desperation.

"Sure would."

"Don't lie, Cliffy."

"I would. I swear."

June 21st I would be fourteen, and Noah would be fifteen August 4th. But I did not feel like a kid, and he didn't look like a kid.

"Hey." I grabbed his arm. "I got an idea, let's take off now. We don't ever have to see our dads again."

"Yeah." He knuckled his eyes. "Let's go."

We showered together, sucking each other in the spray. It was fun and crazy and so real. Realer than anything I had ever done before. As real as the water was wet and warm. His white toes against my yellow ones sent waves of tingles that changed the way my eyes saw. Changed what the water looked like as it pooled around our feet and rained down on us. My mouth on him, his on me, our throats gagging in the push and pleasure. His pubic hair had a black shine, blacker than the night and the stars. Hands soaped, we milked ourselves raw, and squirted on the shower curtains. I felt more than myself, greater than myself. I was all that I could ever be in that moment. I was in love.

We biked to our favorite spot. There, the daffodils had left, and the green of spring became summer. Near the creek, grass filled with dandelions. Bees bounced from yellow head to yellow head. The air swirled with the white seeds of what we called Afro flowers. We set down at the same spot as last time. Noah took off his socks and shoes and waded in. The water was clear and big tadpoles skittered around pebbles and rocks. I watched from our grassy seat. I brought Stowe to go with our potato chips. I pulled it out, but then put it back. We were going to run away before Mr. Coursey's class on Monday. Stowe didn't matter.

And then it hit me.

"Noah, we're not running away, are we?"

He didn't answer. He traced circles on the water's surface with his big toe.

I nearly shouted "You deaf?"

"I heard you."

"You don't want to runaway?"

"No."

"It's because of that girl on the playground?"

"Jasmine? No, I just wanted to do her. I thought she'd let us both. She said I was a Nigger lover."

"And she's a ragweed."

He changed directions and came toward me. "I don't want to run away because..."

"Why not?"

"...uh..."

"It's because of me... Did I...?"

"We're moving back to New York."

"Huh?"

"We're moving back to New York. So we can be with our family. They can help Mom with us and Dad."

I couldn't speak.

"Ari's coming with his dad. My uncle's going to help Mom sell the business."

"But what about us going to Walnut Hills and us living next to each other? What about us being friends forever?"

"Soul brother, soon as we get a big enough place, you can live with us. It's only about seven hundred miles. Greyhound's cheap."

I knew I wasn't going to New York. That we would never see each other again once he left town. I'd be stuck in Finlater forever—the place I couldn't stand or spell.

"Come on, don't cry," he said.

"I don't want you to go."

He plopped down beside me. "You're coming with us. My mom will let you. I know she will."

I locked my arms around him. "Please don't leave. Please don't leave me. You go, I'll, I'll be all alone. I'll die here."

"Don't say that."

"Don't go. Please."

We lay there in the grass, beside the gurgling stream, crying. Though the sun had moved from the peak of day, it was still as bright as the dandelions. Noah fingered his zipper. Soon he rolled on his side and dozed off. I lay there staring at his back, reading my future of longing written on his skin.

I was afraid to let him out of my sight.

kiSs AnD tElL

God, if real, must be mean. Mean to me, especially, maybe for doubting Him in the first place. I realized that I must have believed in God since I now blamed Him for my suffering. All I wanted was to be near Noah. Seven hundred miles between us was what I got—or would soon get. Were there other boys in the world like Noah and me? Boys thumping each other's fingers as they lay in the grass, wondering how to survive without each other?

"SB, you know what? I'm glad we're not running away. I know these aren't slavery times, but Eliza when she ran away didn't have much fun. Hopping ice floes and being hunted by wild dogs."

"Girls shouldn't run away," Noah said. "Well, I guess if you're a slave you should."

"Unless what you're running to is worse."

"How would you know that though?"

"I don't know. Guess you'd have to know somebody who's done it before. I don't." I knew all kinds of folks, but Eliza was my first runaway.

"Me either," Noah said. "Nobody I know has ever done it."

"We'll be the first, pioneering runaways."

"Cool."

"Don't know about you, but I wouldn't mind sleeping outside and wearing the same clothes. Though I guess you'd stink real bad after a while."

Noah laughed, "We wouldn't have to worry about clothes."

His eyes widened. Like he'd solved a riddle, or remembered

something forgotten. He took off running, shouting "Let's go."

At first I thought maybe Elmwood bullies had surrounded us or taken our things. But our things were fine, and we were still alone.

"What's the matter?"

"Just come on."

We biked back to his house. The station wagon wasn't there. He told me to wait, and ran inside. Shortly he returned. He hopped back on, and we took off.

"Where we going?"

"You'll see."

Winton Road went downhill. Not steeply, but sloping just enough for a boost of easy speed. I thought maybe we were going to another of his favorite spots. After what seemed like ten miles, I figured he had a greater purpose.

Spring Grove Avenue was familiar by name, but we went along a cemetery in a direction I'd never been, so I didn't know where we were. Grave markers like rows of teeth gleamed on a hill rising west of us. The road evened out but gradually climbed. Soon Noah's undershirt was soaked with sweat. Cars sped by, their black or white grownup occupants staring at us, sometimes shaking their heads. The kids aboard smiled and waved. It was like we were at the front of a race. I couldn't see Noah's face. All his energy horse-powered us forward. He said nothing, neither did I. I'd take over peddling as soon as he asked. He knew that.

We turned down Hamilton, winding our way downtown. I

saw signs with street names I knew, like Central and Vine, streets that fed into Cincinnati's heart. But I still didn't know where we were exactly. This must be like how it is running away. Like Eliza and Harry felt. You just keep moving, hopping over danger, hoping you end up someplace safe. Hoping you find people to help or take you in and give you safe passage to a better life. It seemed like he'd been peddling for hours as we turned on Central Avenue. We were passing through Over the Rhine by way of the Race street projects. They were tall grimy buildings filled with ghetto trouble. There was a black movie theater where Mom and Mr. Porter sometimes dropped us kids off for a Sunday show, until a shooting happened. Even Dudley, who wasn't afraid of anybody or anything, was nervous around there.

Noah wasn't worried or pretended not to be. He seemed to know exactly how to handle the projects. He peddled down the middle of the street. People shouted at us—"punks," "honkie," "bitches," "Oreos." Somebody threw a soda can from their car. Noah remained unfazed. It was like our future depended on a bus sliding in the snow. I didn't care if we were run over or shot at, it didn't matter. Nothing mattered. Except being with him, now and always.

I could see Union Terminal to my right. Soon Cincinnati Music Hall was just ahead. Central Avenue veered off to the left, heading straight into downtown. Tall buildings of the city rose like a forest. I could see the public library as we crossed an intersection. I looked ahead. Then I knew where Noah was taking us.

We hopped the curb with a bump that threw us off balance.

We toppled over at the entrance to Ben's. The sign Ben's Clothing for Men was busted up. The store entrance was closed with a chain gate. Beyond the gate, the windows were broken, too. Shards of glass littered the entrance.

"Fucking assholes," Noah spat. He fished around in his pockets and produced keys. He fumbled with the the lock until the gate opened. I helped him lift it up enough so he could open the door locks. We pushed the bicycle in and slammed the gate down, locking it from the inside.

We clicked the lights on. The place looked ransacked. Clothes were everywhere, in a big mess. Clothes for every kind of hip man there was. Bellbottoms, pimp pleats and pleat-free pants, suits, red shirts, pointy shoes, and alligator boots.

"This is my dad's store," Noah said, proudly, as if it always looked like this. I figured his pride meant he really cared nothing about this stuff—and probably Mr. Baumgarten didn't either—but it was Noah's dad's place all the same.

He turned to me. "Is there something in particular you'd like, sir?"

Noah put the radio on. We stripped down to underwear. We tried on everything, with James Brown, Aretha Franklin, Marvin Gaye, Curtis Mayfield, and Stevie Wonder singing us on. We turned into pimps, undertakers, holy-rollers, and businessmen. We hustled between racks, monkeyed at the coats section, and did the cha-cha-cha near the cash register. Noah showed me the Charleston and the foxtrot. We changed at the spot where we found clothes, leaving a rumpled, colorful trail behind, with our laughter.

There was soda pop in the refrigerator and some old potato chips. We downed it all and nothing tasted finer. Noah, a big green feather sticking out of his hat, fell backwards after a huge belch.

I took my fly cap off and launched it across the room. We wrestled around on the floor, making an even bigger mess.

"I used to love working down here. In the summer, Dad would let me sometimes. I'd get to ring up purchases."

"Too bad your mom has to get rid of everything."

"Yeah," he said. "Mom doesn't think so. She hates this place. But Dad didn't. He really loved being down here. He never got along with his dad, and he loved Uncle Ben more than anybody. Uncle Ben played the saxophone. He said they used to play together—that was before Nam and my dad's hands got shot off. My mom went to law school here, that's how they met—well, through our New York families. They went back to New York and I was born there, but when Uncle Ben got sick, Dad wanted to come back. And Mom liked it here, so we did. Dad went back to this store that he loved so much. Uncle Ben got better with us here, well, Dad really—I think he had prostate problems, I don't remember. Anyway, he'd always wanted to go to Israel, and so Dad took him. It was a car bomb that killed him. They were at a café. Dad went to the restroom, and boom. Everybody slaughtered. He survived by climbing out a window. My dad really went to pieces after that. Why so many bad things happen to my dad? He's the best, Cliffy. I don't understand what kinda God sticks it to a good man like him?"

"My grandma says, God has reasons that reason will never know."

"Or there isn't a God. Uncle Ben didn't believe in God. I don't, either."

"Why did he want to go to Israel then?"

"Because he's a Jew. He was born a Jew."

Guess it was like being born black. Grandpa Pleasant always said he wanted to see Africa. Maybe it was the same.

"My dad was so happy here. People just come by to talk and listen to records. Even now, if we put the gates up, some of the old men around here will come by and play their music, or play records. Funny thing is, he just didn't sell clothes. People stole left and right."

He pulled from his pocket a pair of red underwear. "Ugh," he said, and threw them across the room.

"Soul brother, I was thinking, we could stay here. We could just move in. Nobody'd even know. Wouldn't that be cool?"

"Until we got hungry. I wouldn't want to go for food around here."

"We could go down to the Ohio River, and we could fish. It's not that far away."

"Like Huck and Jim."

"It's fun. Sometimes me and my dad would go fishing. He had a friend with a boat, an old blues singer over in Covington, and we'd take it out..."

"Okay, let's just stay here."

And we did.

By 9 P.M. I felt starved. Leaving so impetuously, we had no money. We wrestled with the safe. Noah thought there was a wad of cash in it, but he didn't know the combination. We gave up and danced some more. We piled clothes on the floor and stomped them down until we had a bed. Then we lay down.

"I always told Dad to get a TV."

"A TV would be nice."

"We don't need a TV, though. Not really."

"No, we don't, but..."

"We can do all kinds of things other than watch TV," Noah grinned.

"Like what?"

Our lips touched. So did the rest of our bodies, even during our sleep.

Next morning, Noah said he wanted us to go someplace. For some reason I thought he had a pool hall or some other kind of place of mischief in mind, but I was wrong. We walked just two blocks before arriving at a big blockish brick building with a bright circle of stained glass high above the entrance.

"Where's this?"

"It's a synagogue. You wanna be a Jew? Well today, at least for a few minutes, you get to be one."

"Really."

"Yeah. We need money and so I figured maybe we'd get some here. My dad used to be friends with the rabbi."

"Won't they call your mom and tell her you were here?"

"Yeah, you got a point."

We wavered at the entrance for a minute or so. I wondered, whatever Noah's intentions, if the Jewish God wouldn't have a problem with us cocksuckers and butt fuckers coming in together, smelling of sex and love.

"I don't know."

"Oh, come on. Let's go in anyway. Maybe there's money on the floor or a donation box left out."

"You gonna rob a church?"

"No, and it's a synagogue."

"You're going to rob a synagogue?"

"No."

"I'm not going in if you planning to do something like that."

"I'm not, I promise. What do you take me for, a thug?"

We pushed through the huge double entry doors, then past a curtain that seemed to hang from forty feet in the air. It was empty, not a soul in sight. It was also dark and cooler inside—so little morning sunlight was there to warm it up, just the colored light passing through the stained glass window I saw from outside, holding a rainbow over the pews. It wasn't like St. Simon at all— our humble shanty of a church—but more like the Methodist church we went to with Miss Glodine once before.

We passed through what Noah described as what used to be the men's side of the synagogue.

"I know, it's like Jim Crow for Jews."

"Maybe you shouldn't say bad things in here? I mean…"

"Afraid a thunderbolt will take us out?"

"Or maybe other bad things…"

"You're right."

We cautiously walked to a pew toward the front of the congregation area. We sat down and Noah bowed his head and whispered.

Mi she-bei-rach a-vo-tei-nu,

M'-kor ha-b'ra-cha l'-i-mo-tei-nu

M'-kor ha-b'ra-cha l'-a-vo-tei-nu

r'fu-a sh'-lei-ma

Before lowering my head, more out of respect than anything else, I looked up at the brightness above, colored red and blue and orange, and felt soothed and warmer, even though it wasn't shining directly on us, with the light floating just above the gloom. It was weird to be here with no other people around, but somehow I knew it was better that it was just us and the Jew God, or so I wanted to believe.

There was a slight clattering sound, and then the thunderous roar of the temple organ coming to life, with sharp, "Count-Dracula" notes.

Noah leapt up from his seat.

"Let's get outta here. I hate that thing."

This was a sign from the Jew God. I loved organs. Maybe

proof that I could be a Jew.

Outside, we walked back to our own little sanctuary.

"My dad used to come here, just before the really bad times would mess him up. His friend the rabbi died last year, too, right before Uncle Ben—and it was like a dial had been turned up on his sadness. He always joked that he was a bad Jew until the sadness turned him to an even worse one, which was how he became a real Jew. Go figure."

"Were you praying?"

"Yeah. I just asked God to heal my father. I don't even believe all this stuff, I think. I just don't know what else to do."

Seemed like everybody got religious during bad times, pick your God.

"Did you hear my prayer?"

"No." He grinned sheepishly at me.

I put my arms around him. "I prayed for the Jew God to not hate me for thinking about you all the time. And then I prayed that if the Jew God wouldn't let me be a Jew, that he would at least let me be in love with one."

"You think he heard?"

"Does the Jewish God speak English?"

"I think so, and even jive, too." Noah laughed at me. "I know how my dad felt about Julio. I love you."

"You do?" I whispered.

"Yeah. You?"

"As sure as I know how to spell Finlater."

He knew. "And how do you spell Finlater?"

"The same way you do. The right way."

"I love you, Noah Ben Baumgarten."

By noon, I ran to a White Castle's we passed on the bike. We had found five bucks in change in the office desk and on the floor of the store. I got sausage and egg sandwiches, pancakes, coffee, and cinnamon buns. We pigged out. He'd chew some sandwich and I'd put my mouth to his and finish it off. I'd always thought you could get cooties from kissing, but I didn't care. Breakfast never tasted so good. With music blasting, we decided we were heading for the river. I had never seen the river up close before.

There was a loud knock on the front door. It sounded like a stick was banging it.

We looked at each other, suddenly afraid. Noah scampered toward the stereo, turning it down. He told me to follow him. He grabbed the bike and we made for the backdoor. Noah fumbled with the lock and finally pushed it open. Guns greeted us. Two big policemen stared at me.

"WHOOOOA. Officer Packert, it's Noah. Remember?"

The officer flicked at a mole on the tip of his sunburned nose. "We were passing by. I heard music and thought we'd check it out."

"Just me and my friend Cliffy cleaning up the place."

"I heard your pa is sick."

"Yeah, but he's better now."

"Your ma know you down here?"

"Sure." Noah stared down at the floor. The other officer had a mustache like sewing needles.

"And you live in Elmwood, don't you? That's a long, dangerous way for two kids on a bike, especially down here."

"Not so bad," Noah said.

"How's about we call her. What's the number?"

Noah gave the number—the right number!—and Officer Packert got patched through using his walkie-talkie. "Mrs. Baumgarten, it's Police Officer Packert, I'm at your husband's place of business and your son said... Not since yesterday, huh?... No, they're fine... Yes, this is a rough area for them to be biking through... I hope your husband gets better... That's too bad."

He hung up.

"Noah, your mom's on her way."

"Thanks a lot."

We changed back into our clothes while Officer Packert thumbed through leather jackets. "Nigger rags," he said. Then he looked at me. "Sorry."

I turned away.

Noah said, "Yeah, we just give the people what they want. Not enough variety in the white-trash look."

"Okay, smart mouth. You got five minutes."

It wasn't long before Mrs. Baumgarten ordered us into the car. She chatted with Officer Packert for a couple of minutes, and then pounced into the driver's seat, flipping her glasses back. But she didn't yell at Noah. Tear-filled eyes stared at him instead, in shock and hurt.

"Noah, I love and miss Daddy, too. Really really badly. You have no idea. But you wouldn't like if I just up and left for New York without telling you, would you?"

It seemed not a question but a statement of fact. Noah shook his head no.

"Never do this again, Noah." She wiped at her eyes with a tissue.

"Okay, Mom," he said. "I'm sorry." Then he climbed over the front seat and kissed her. "I'm really sorry. I won't do it again. I just miss Dad. Why can't he be alright?"

They cried in each other's arms. I watched, wishing more than anything to be with him and Mrs. Baumgarten forever. Just the three of us.

284

The end was near. I could feel it.

At their house, Mrs. Baumgarten sent Noah ahead.

"Cliffy, I know Noah put you up to running away and you were just being the good friend that you are. So you tell me, should I tell your mother about this?"

"No, ma'am."

"Why not?"

Her dark eyes held me in place as we stopped along the sidewalk.

"Because, because..."

"I need a better reason."

"Because... I'll never be allowed outside Finlater again."

FINAL ACT

The show must go on. After worrying his mother so, we focused on our "theatrics." Our performance would be right after Sunday evening supper. It was 3 P.M. when we got back to his house. We practiced the scene with Mr. Shelby telling Uncle Tom he's being sold to settle a debt. We giggled at the craziness of it, but in the back of my mind I kept thinking what it would be like to be separated from Noah. Is this what Uncle Tom felt as all that he loved in the world was about to be taken from him, without his permission, with him unable to do anything about it?

I pulled myself together—curtain was in an hour.

First stop was makeup. Leeza had been practicing on her dolls.

We'd also brought along clothes from Ben's. While Leeza made Noah up as Mr. Shelby, I shredded a pair of bellbottoms and a teeshirt for my role as Uncle Tom.

Mrs. Baumgarten knocked on Noah's bedroom door.

"Cliffy, I haven't heard from your mom. Maybe she didn't get things straightened out with your dad. Why don't you call and ask if you can stay tonight, too? Use the hall phone, sweetie."

I darted into the hall just as Mrs. Baumgarten was going in her bedroom.

"Mrs. Baumgarten," I called out.

"Yes, Cliffy."

"I'm glad you like my mom. You do know her?"

Mrs. Baumgarten smiled.

"Don't you?"

She seemed to think about it before answering. "Just in passing, sweetie."

"And Mrs. Baumgarten, don't worry, I can get home by myself. There's no Klan"—I stupidly smiled as I said it—"or even Palestinians in the park. I'd kill 'em if there were."

She looked pained. Her fingers suddenly touched my cheek. "You have no idea what you're talking about."

What had I said? "I mean…"

"Cliffy, there's enough killing in the world already. Now go call your mother."

It was Corey who answered the phone.

"Where's Mom?"

"She's upstairs."

"Speak up, I can't hear you."

"I said she's upstairs, and I don't think she can talk right now."

"Why? Something wrong?"

"She's gone off the deep end and is packing Dad's stuff."

"What?"

"She's throwing him out."

"Who?"

"Dad, dodo bird, can't you hear right!"

"Dad?"

"Yeah, Dad. He's in jail right now. Boy, you missed a good one."

Dudley and Dad had had their fight. Dudley and Corey went to the ponykeg for pork rinds. Dudley caught Dad hitting on Maybelline. He saw her sitting in the Thunderbird and just went psycho. The police got them. Dudley was in the hospital and Dad at the precinct in Avondale.

"Cliffy, you wouldn't believe it—Dad cracked Dudley's ribs with a punch like Joe Frazier, but Dudley, he put up a fight. Busted his nose, and before Dad stomped him on the ground, Dudley ripped Dad's shirt off, you know the silver one. "

"Whatcha do?"

"I ran home. I told Mom. It ain't right."

"Nothing's right." Except Dudley—he had been right all along. "Tell Mom I'm gonna stay the night and go to school from here in the morning. I'll be home after school."

"Cliffy, I don't think she cares right now. I wish I had me some honkie friends I could stay with."

I hung up and returned to Noah's room.

Leeza didn't know what a slave master looked like. Noah, in her hands, looked like Rod Stewart the rock star.

Somehow, although all new to me, this seemed normal compared to what was happening in my house.

Isaac shouted, "Come on, the audience is getting rektless."

"It's restless, Zacky. Go take your seat," Noah yelled back. Then, to me, "Your mom say you could stay?"

I nodded.

We finished our makeup and costumes and trooped down to

the living room. We did our act under a stage rigged with flashlights, done by Mrs. Baumgarten and Isaac.

"But massa," I blubbered, upon hearing the news that I was being sold away and separated from my "fambly."

We couldn't keep a straight face, and yet deep down I knew there was nothing funny in the funny-sounding words. And Mrs. Baumgarten's stern face proved the point. We struggled through the difficult dialect, laughing all the way.

Isaac was the only one who applauded.

"I guess your Laurel and Hardy rendition is creative license," Mrs. Baumgarten said when we were done. "But the very idea that you would mock and laugh at other people's misery and pain just breaks my heart."

"It was the words, Mom."

"What are there but words! You two, especially you two, should know better. Ask yourself, where is my humanity? Where is my compassion? Selfish, foolish boys."

And she rushed away to the kitchen. It was hard to know whether she was still mad over our botched runaway attempt, or worse. During dinner, her eyes didn't meet mine and, it seemed to me, avoided Noah's, too. I kept hearing her voice—Where is my humanity? Where is my compassion? I wondered if it was her humanity and compassion that reasoned with Noah over running away without a word or phone call, instead of slapping him through the floor, as my mom would have done. I then thought of my poor mom, broke up over a worthless man she couldn't help herself but love, even against the good sense God gave her. Even to the very end.

Out of the corner of my eye, I watched Mrs. Baumgarten, in her quiet simmering, struggling over lasagna and tossed salad, and I wondered what she would do if she knew about Noah and me, us boys in love. Maybe she did know, not the details—maybe she couldn't handle the details—but just enough to know that we were in love.

When Noah and me were alone, I said, "Your mom's right. We shouldn't have made a mockery. It's not funny."

"It is funny. It's the way we did it."

"It's not funny, and we shouldn't have done it that way."

"Who cares?"

"Mr. Coursey will give us an F."

"And I'll write a nice little letter to him about you seeing him sucking cock down at the railroad tracks."

I thought about fat awful Mr. Coursey. As much as I disliked him, us being the cause of ruining his life would not stand.

"No," I said. "It isn't right. I don't wanna tell lies on him."

"I thought you said…"

"I made it all up. Just to see what you'd do."

"You know what your punishment is for P-R-E-V-A-R-I-C-A-T-I-O-N, don't you?" he snickered.

B-L-O-W-J-O-B.

We wrestled down to the mattress, shamelessly laughing and carrying on with his family one locked door away. The music blasting so loud that his mother finally banged the door for us to keep it down. The odd things was, Mrs. Baumgarten never left my thoughts. Had she seen us, heard us, or just read the looks I gave her son? I didn't tell Noah what I suspected about his mom, fearing that he might just blow up in her face or something. I limited what I had to say to what I felt in my heart. Love and lies.

"My mother wants me to come home."

"I thought she said it was okay?"

"She didn't. It's my brother Dudley. He's hurt."

"What's happened?"

"Ambushed in Evanston."

Anything was possible with Dudley, so I let Noah think it was gang-related. I couldn't face Mrs. Baumgarten again, and so I told him that I didn't want to burden his mom with driving me home. He in turn let her believe we were going for a walk in the neighborhood. Shortly, we were biking to the park that would lead me home to Finlater. I clung to his body so tight he could hardly peddle.

At our usual break-off point, we held hands, and then we kissed. I knew I would see him again and again and then never again, but somehow right now seemed so final, so ultimate, like neither of us would ever be the same the second we parted.

He pointed up at the sky. "Maybe that's where we should've run away to—the moon. Huh, Cliffy, the moon, the Milkyway, huh, Cliffy?"

Just then, I could see the flow of the constellations clearly.

But just as suddenly, I didn't know what I was looking at. It might as well have been Noah's name in the sky of my heart, now shattered into fine sparkly dust that didn't mean anything.

"You know what's funny," I said. "I was scared to run away, but I would have… with you. I would have." The hurt grabbed me in the gut. "Your mom thinks you put me up to running off with you, but I was always the one for real. Not you. You just talk." The bitter taste of disappointment seeped into the corners of my lips. "I would have, I swear. But not you, Noah. You wouldn't have. That's what I know."

He didn't disagree. Instead, his eyes pooling up, he sputtered, "I wish you wouldn't cry. We'll figure it out. You'll see. My mom and dad'll help us. They will. I promise."

The words I couldn't say were written all over me— YOU DON'T LOVE ME THE WAY I DO YOU. If only he could read me.

I ran through the woods certain of only one thing. My mother needed me. I blanked on what I could do for her now, with her love all twisted up. I was afraid. I was mad. But I belonged to her.

I loved her first before I knew about love.

tHE End

To Georgianna Ruff,
mommy dearest.

ACKNOWLEDGMENTS

Many thanks for the love and patience of the special ones holding my hand for the long haul. Above all, my angel in this life, Irving Marshall. Brilliant, beautiful, beloved: Beryl Meyer, Gabri Christa, Sasha Dees, Judy White, Kwy Brown, Luther E. Vann, Ann T. Greene, Fiona Ip, and dearests Tanya Ruff-Gure and the little ones. The aunts—Carolyn and Mary—and Uncle Albert, one of the finest men I've ever known. Unparalleled editor and gentleman: Msr. Claude-Albert Saucier. Invaluable readers: Marcella Amlie, Stephen Kent Jones, G. Winston James, Antonio Calvo, and cousin Carolyn Gentry. The artists: Michael Opalski and especially Don Joseph for the book's inimitable look. And lastly, the spirits: Grandpa and Grandma Beatty, and my greatest love of all (so far!), the late Kenneth Mooney.

Also by Shawn Stewart Ruff

Go the Way Your Blood Beats
An Anthology of Lesbian and Gay Fiction
by African American Writers

QUOTE
" EDITIONS "

First Edition
Copyright ©2008 Shawn Stewart Ruff